Love Is Random Too

# Hook Up or Break Up

## Love Is Random Too

### KENDALL ADAMS

HarperTempest
*An Imprint of* HarperCollins*Publishers*
A PARACHUTE PRESS BOOK

HarperTempest is an imprint of HarperCollins Publishers.

Hook Up or Break Up: Love Is Random Too
Copyright © 2006 by Parachute Publishing, LLC.

www.harperteen.com

Library of Congress Catalog Card Number: 2006920319
ISBN-10: 0-06-088563-7—ISBN-13: 978-0-06-088563-2

❖

First HarperTempest edition, 2006

Love Is Random Too

one

"I'm going to do it. I'm going to ask Josh Marx out," I announced. "Today."

My best friend, Kerri Lawrence, who knew me better than anyone, lowered her dark sunglasses and squinted at me. She looked ready to call for help.

"You feeling all right?" she asked.

"Sure! Fine! Great, actually! Seriously! Never better!"

Okay, so maybe I sounded a bit manic. My voice was freakishly shrill, and my forced grin bordered on painful. I curled my bare toes into the grass and tried to tone it down.

"I mean, I'm cool."

"You're going to ask out Josh Marx," Kerri said finally. "You."

"Yes, me. Right now. Or, within the next five minutes."

That was when Kerri cracked up laughing. She leaned back against the leg of her lifeguard chair and held her stomach. She almost doubled over. A middle-aged woman shot us a pissed-off scowl and moved her swimmies-sporting kid to the beach towel on her far side, as if our psycho tendencies were going to rub off on him or something.

"Kerri!" I said through my teeth.

I hate it when people laugh at me. Absolutely hate it. It's probably my least favorite thing in the world. And Kerri knows this. Yet there she was, gasping for air, laughing until we were both red in the face.

"I'm sorry. It's just, I—" But she couldn't finish the sentence. That's how hard she was laughing.

People all around us were starting to stare. We were standing near the edge of the water at The Mill—the big man-made pond that is technically "The Garden Hills Old Mill Town Pool and Recreation Area"—and the place was jam-packed. Every year the citizens of my little suburban town of Garden Hills, Maryland, came out of the woodwork for the end-of-summer blowout, attracted, apparently, by the promise of free ice cream and face painting. Basically my entire hometown was there to witness this little spectacle if they so chose.

"Sorry. I'm sorry," Kerri said, getting control of herself.

She stood up to her full height, a good four inches taller than me. With her red life-guarding bathing suit set against her dark, oiled skin she looked like a regular from *Baywatch*. She even had the breasts for it—developed practically overnight in the summer between sixth and seventh grade, while the rest of us were still flat. I, of course, still am.

Which may be why no one's ever bothered trying to feel me up. But that could all change if everything worked out with Josh Marx. He could be the first guy to—

Whoa, boy. Okay. Shouldn't think about that just now. I had to keep as level a head as possible, and it was already twisting off its axis *without* adding my embarrassing lack of sexual experience into the equation. Josh Marx was, shall we say, light-years ahead of me in that department. As were all the girls he'd ever hooked up with.

"It's just . . . Quinn, do you know how long I've been listening to you say that?" Kerri asked with a sympathetic smile. "Like, *five years.*"

"Well, this time I'm actually going to do it," I told her. The butterflies that had been bothering me all day went zinging through my stomach like hornets on speed. "Do you realize how many times I've talked to him this summer? Eight! Nine, if you count the first one."

"The one where he came up to you at the skate park and told you he liked your new board, but you were unable to formulate a response through all your love-struck shock?" Kerri said, crossing her arms over her chest.

Oh, yeah. I'd forgotten I told her about that.

My face burned. "You're mocking me."

"No! I'm not! I'm sorry," Kerri said again.

Everything was different because of those eight or nine times. I mean, he'd smiled at me. He'd looked me in the eye on several occasions. He'd noticed the original artwork on my board. Was it possible that, finally, after years of my pining in silent misery, Josh Marx was actually thinking about me? Was it possible that it was finally, *finally* my turn?

"The thing is, I *have* to do it," I told her, picking at the black sweatband on my wrist. "It's senior year. If I don't do it now, I'm never gonna do it. And then I'll always be wondering what if."

"Okay. If you're sure . . ." Kerri said.

I felt a sudden swoop of insecurity. "What?"

Kerri eyed me uncertainly. "I don't know. What if he turns out not to be that great? What if he isn't the Mr. Perfect you've been pining for all this time? Won't you be crushed?"

"Kerri!"

How could she say this to me? How could she say this to me now of all moments? Was she *trying* to freak me out?

"I just don't think he's all that great. He's so cocky," Kerri said. "Plus he's kind of a slut," she added matter-of-factly.

My face burned. "Okay, I know he's gone out with a lot of girls—"

"And hooked up with ten thousand more," Kerri pointed out—a little too enthusiastically, if you asked me.

"*But,* maybe that's just because he's looking for the *right* one," I said.

Kerri smiled and sighed. "The eternal optimist. Well, fine then. I'm all for it. Go talk to him. Hey! Maybe if you guys start going out, we'll finally be able to talk about something else!"

"Ha-ha," I said flatly.

"Although it would probably just get worse, because instead of daydreams, you'd have actual details," Kerri said. "Details to dissect and analyze and talk about over and over—"

"Why do I even tell you anything?" I asked her.

"Because you love me," she said with a shrug.

"Lawrence! Break's over!" shouted Tim Walsh, head lifeguard and power freak.

"Okay!" Kerri shouted back.

She leaned in and gave me a sweaty, suntan-lotiony hug. "Really. Good luck. I'm rooting for you," she said sincerely.

"Thanks," I said.

That's the thing about Kerri. Ninety-nine percent of what she says is sarcastic, but she always manages to get serious when it counts. She turned and climbed up onto her lifeguard chair again, relieving Danny Chazotte. Kerri crossed her long legs and twirled her whistle, scanning the pond.

I sighed. If I had even one iota of her confidence, I would have asked out Josh back in eighth grade when I first saw him do a handstand in the middle of the hallway. He held it for ten seconds longer than anyone thought was humanly possible, and when he stood up again, his hair flopped into his face.

What happened next had replayed in my mind so many times I wouldn't be surprised if it was actually physically burned into my brain. Josh flipped his bangs away from his face, looked right at me with those insanely blue eyes, and smiled. At me. That was the moment when all other guys ceased to exist.

"Are you going?" Kerri asked from above, never taking her eyes off the water.

My stomach turned. I reached back to tighten my pony-tail and smoothed the front of my cargo shorts, which I wore over my plain black one-piece.

"I'm going," I said.

"Good. For a minute there I thought you might be wussing out," she replied.

"Hey. Wussing out is not in my vocabulary today."

Yeah, right.

I took a deep breath and forced myself to start walking. Josh was a lifeguard at the pond, too, but his shift had ended half an hour ago. Not that I know his schedule by heart or anything. I'm not a stalker. I just happened to notice when he climbed down from his chair and went into the office next to the snack bar to punch out. But he was still here somewhere. No one leaves the end-of-summer party before the nine o'clock fireworks. We in Garden Hills are slaves to tradition that way.

My skin sizzled as I rounded the picnic tables and headed for the long, low building that held the changing room, snack bar, first-aid area, and office. The very thought of talking to Josh made every cell in my body go psycho.

The thing about Josh is that he's perfect. And I'm not just saying that. He's one of those people who can hang out with every crowd at school, and no one thinks it's even the tiniest bit weird. He's on the football team, he stars in all the winter musicals, he boards like an X Games veteran. He's even nice to the geeks who, let's face it, aren't even nice to each other. Plus he's gorgeous. Like I-got-my-own-show-on-the-WB-even-though-I-can't-act-to-save-my-life gorgeous.

Except that he *can* act.

Anyway, because of this perfection, everyone else I know has been in love with him at one point or another. Even Kerri had that one delusional month in eighth grade when she followed him around like a puppy dog, and I spent every waking moment swearing to God that I would clean my room every day if He would just not let Kerri have him. Luckily Kerri got kissed by Nick Corso at Janet Leone's Valentine's party and forgot all about Josh.

I've had to watch him go through an endless stream of girlfriends: cheerleaders, choir chicks, Glossies (those girls who carry the latest *Vogue* with them everywhere even though it's thick and heavy enough to make you hunch-backed), even a couple of my softball teammates. But I've always known—*always*—that if I could just get up the guts to talk to him for more than ten seconds, he would see that I was the girl he was meant to be with. He would see how thoughtful and talented and excellent I am and fall madly, incoherently in love with me.

And having a boyfriend would also mean my parents would stop asking me if I was ever going to bring a guy home, and my little brother Jack could stop calling me "the dateless loser."

I *so* love my brother. Not.

"Yo, Donny!"

"Hey, Corey."

Corey Haskell is one of my boarding buddies and also my co-chair of the homecoming committee this year. Every year homecoming takes place at the end of September, so once school starts we'll be spending even more time together than usual. Not only will we be planning the homecoming dance, but also the Spirit Show—a yearly competition in which each class puts on a skit and the whole school votes for the best one.

Corey is also the president of the senior class and has a nickname for every single person he knows. Mine's "Donny" because my last name is Donohue—not because he thinks of me as one of the guys. I hope. Of course, *Quinn* is a boy's name, too. My parents pretty much doomed me from birth.

"Whaddup?" Corey asked, taking a huge chunk off the top of his swirly cone.

"Have you seen Josh Marx anywhere?" I asked.

"Yeah. He went around that corner approximately two-point-five seconds ago," Corey told me, pointing. "Why?"

Once again my face reddened. "I'll . . . tell ya later."

Corey shrugged and moved off with his ice cream cone. I turned and took a deep breath. This was it. All I had to do was get around that corner. There would be no turning back. This was the first moment of the rest of my life.

I rolled my shoulders back, ignored the hornets that were now attacking my heart, and stepped around the corner of the snack bar.

Instantly all the hornets dropped dead and crashed to the wet concrete with the rest of my insides.

There was Josh Marx, not ten feet away from me, with his tongue down Danielle DeLaurentis's throat and his hand sliding up under her tank top. Her curly hair was all smashed up against the rock wall behind her, and she was running her fingers up and down Josh's back.

*Danielle DeLaurentis? Danielle DeLaurentis? Are you kidding me? The girl puts the* skank *in* skanky. *She wears purple glitter nail polish and paints on a fake mole! Is this some kind of sick joke?*

And then it hit me like a skate ramp to the face. Kerri was right. Josh Marx *was* a slut! He hadn't been thinking about me at all. Those nine times he'd talked to me had clearly meant nothing. I was the definition of *pathetic*.

*Go! Go now, you idiot!*

My flight reflex finally kicked in, and I turned around, but not before this new and disgusting image was burned into my brain for all eternity. Ugh. Two seconds ago I was thinking about what it would be like to have those very hands sliding up *my* shirt, and now I had seen them groping Danielle DeLaurentis. Suddenly I felt gross. Gross and stupid and scrawny and flat.

I was never going to waste another second thinking about Josh Marx again. Not ever.

# two

"I can't believe it! Danielle DeLaurentis?" I ranted, following Kerri up the creaky stairs to her bedroom. "She's such a ho-bag."

"I told you so!" Kerri singsonged. She never misses a chance to say *I told you so*.

"He could do so much better!" I said.

"Like you, perhaps?" she asked, glancing over her shoulder.

"No. Not like me," I replied. I wasn't thinking about Josh anymore. I wasn't!

"Yeah, sure," Kerri scoffed. "Cuz you are so obviously over him."

She pushed open the door to her bedroom where she had laid out five prospective first-day-of-school outfits on her double bed. Shopping bags were lined up on the floor, full of things Kerri had either yet to unpack from her shopping spree or stuff she was going to return. Kerri was a master returner. She hardly ever tried stuff on in the store. She had this whole theory about having to see the clothes on in natural light. I never understood it.

"So, what do you think?" she asked, studying her choices.

I dropped into her desk chair and started spinning around. "I think I'm never going to have a boyfriend. This is it, Ker. I'm done. Clearly me and guys just don't mix."

"So, lesbianism?" she suggested.

I stopped spinning and flushed. "I don't think so."

Kerri rolled her eyes and dropped the belt she was considering. "Quinn, when are you going to realize that Josh Marx is not the only munchable guy in the world? He's not even the only munchable guy in our *school*. In fact, ever since he groped Danielle DeLaurentis, of all people, in a public place, I'm starting to think he's not munchable at all."

"What's your point?" I groaned, tipping my head back to stare at the ceiling.

"My point is, there are hundreds of great guys out there just dying to hook up with a hottie like you," Kerri said.

"I am *not* a hottie," I told her, lifting my head up. Whoa. Head rush.

"God, Quinn! You are so blind!" Kerri wailed. "Even without products you blow half the senior-class girls out of the water."

"So, what? I should just go up to some random guy and say, 'Hey! Wanna hook up?'" I joked.

"*Yes!*" Kerri cried. Then she actually dropped down to her knees in front of my chair and grabbed my wrists. Did I mention that Kerri can be kind of a drama queen? "Do you have any idea how happy that would make me?"

I laughed. "I wouldn't even know who to ask." If I ever had the guts to do it.

Kerri's eyes lit up, and I knew from experience that she had a plan.

"I have a plan!" she said.

See?

She jumped up and opened one of the built-in cabinets next to her bed. From the mess of crap inside, she pulled out her junior yearbook. She flipped to the section with our class photos and flattened it on the floor.

"Scissors," she said, holding a hand out to me.

I handed over a pair of purple-handled scissors. "What're you gonna do?"

"This."

And just like that she started chopping up her yearbook.

"What are you *doing*?" I asked.

"Please. It's not like I've even looked at it since I got it," she said. She was so focused, it was almost scary. "Besides, this is much more important."

"I don't get it," I said, my brow knitting as scrap after scrap of glossy paper fluttered to the floor.

"Oh, you will," Kerri told me.

She worked for a few minutes in silence while I twirled around on her chair some more. Finally the clipping stopped and I paused, waiting for the room to quit spinning. When I looked down again, squares of paper were strewn all over the floor.

"Okay, pick three," Kerri said.

"Pick three what?" I asked.

"Guys!" she replied, as if I were some kind of moron.

"What?"

"I cut out the top fifty most eligible bachelors from our class," she said, looking very pleased with herself. She pointed down at the photo squares. "They're all there, facedown. You are going to pick three of them and ask them all out. Guaranteed one of them will be your date to the homecoming dance. *Guaranteed.*"

My stomach thwumped over and lay there like roadkill. She might as well have announced that she'd entered me in the Miss Teen U.S.A. pageant.

"Uh, no," I said.

"What? It's the perfect plan!" Kerri said, mixing up the slick scraps of faces.

"For who?" I asked her. "Kerri, you've known me since kindergarten. When have I ever talked to a strange guy?"

"That's the *beauty* of the plan!" Kerri said. "It'll force you to get over your stupid shyness problem."

"Oh, thanks," I said dryly.

"I'm serious, Quinn," Kerri said. She did look serious. "We're going away to college next year. What're you gonna do, never talk to a guy?"

I clucked my tongue and sighed, but deep down everything inside me went haywire. That was actually one of my biggest fears. That I'd never get over my choke tendency, and I'd spend my entire life boyfriendless and alone, working some lame-ass job where you don't have to talk to anyone. See, I'm great in groups—like motivating the softball team or leading homecoming meetings—but I suck one-on-one. I can't stand it when someone expects me to look them in the eye and talk to them about myself or pretty much anything else. I get totally tongue-tied being put on the spot like that. I don't even want to *think* about what's going to happen on college interviews. Stick a fork in me now.

"You've gotta do this," Kerri said.

"Kerri, there's just no way," I said.

"Come on! You can't spend your entire life wondering what would have happened if you just stuck your neck out there," Kerri said.

"Uh, hello? Look what happened the last time I stuck my neck out there?" I said, wide-eyed.

"All the more reason for you to do this now! Get right back out there!" Kerri said. "Don't let Josh Marx and Danielle DeSkank ruin your entire romantic future!"

I had to laugh. Kerri must have seen it as a sign of my caving, because she leaned back with her lips in a triumphant twist. And maybe I was, a little. I mean, it would be next to impossible for me to ask random guys out, but what was the alternative—to stay boyfriendless and virginal forever? Hardly appealing.

"Now pick," Kerri said.

I sighed and sat down across from her on the floor, the array of mauled faces between us. Slowly I slid three scraps of paper toward me. I stared at each, wondering who was on the other side.

Kerri was practically drooling. "So? Let's see!"

I took a deep breath and held it. I flipped over the first picture.

Owen Meyer.

"Oooh. The strong, silent type," Kerri said with a grin.

Silent, definitely. In fact, I wasn't sure I'd ever heard Owen Meyer speak, and I'd known him since we were five. He was the star of the Garden Hills High basketball team, but whenever he was on the bench, he threw a towel over his head and hunkered down, just waiting until he was put back in. And any time he got called on in class, he turned all blotchy and slumped down in his chair, muttering under his breath until the teacher gave up. Most of them stopped calling on him about two weeks into the school year to avoid all the awkwardness. In some ways he kind of reminded me of me.

"Who's next?" Kerri asked.

I flipped over picture number two.

Corey Haskell.

"Aw, yeah!" Kerri said.

"Oh, no," I replied. "No fair! He shouldn't even be in there!"

"Why not? You guys are already friends," Kerri said. "Sometimes it's good to be friends first."

"And sometimes it's a disaster. I can't ask him out! He'll laugh in my face!"

"No he won't," Kerri replied.

"Besides, he's still hung up on Elena," I reminded her. "Everyone knows that."

"Well, then *you'll* just have to help him get over her," she said with a glint in her eyes.

I scoffed. Like that was going to happen. Elena Marlowe and Corey Haskell had been the couple of the century until she heartlessly dumped him last year for Logan Arnott. Corey hadn't been himself for months, and we all knew that if Elena ever went back to him, Corey would fall at her feet in thanks. I couldn't ask out a guy who was in love with someone else. Especially not someone who looked like Elena Marlowe. Can you say *supermodel*?

"Forget it. I'm picking someone else."

I reached for the pile, but Kerri smacked the back of my hand. "Uh-uh! I made up the rules! You have to go with the first three you picked."

"Did you just hit me?" I asked.

Kerri bit her lip. "Sorry."

Time to get on with it. I turned over the third picture. Nothing could be worse than asking out Corey.

The last guy was Max Eastwood.

"Sweet!" Kerri said.

I kind of had to agree with her there. Max Eastwood was beyond hot. Last year he'd come to our school from Australia as part of an exchange program. Then in June, instead of going home to the beach and the kangaroos, he'd decided to stay for senior year. He was going to live with some random family member already here in the States. Rumor had it that he was after a soccer scholarship for college and that he was in love with America.

I stared at the three photos. Corey grinned up at me. Max was all smoldering eyes. Owen looked as if someone had just nailed his feet to the ground. What the hell was I doing?

"How am I supposed to date three guys at once?" I asked, trying to find any hole in this plan. "Won't they find out about each other?"

"Ah, that's the beauty of going to an overpopulated school. These guys barely even *know* each other," she said.

"Corey knows everyone," I reminded her.

"True. But he has to, politician that he is. But he's not *friends* with these guys," she said. "By the time any of them finds out about the other ones, you'll already have picked one. No harm. No foul."

Wow. She'd really thought this through. Or, more likely, she was making it up on the spot. I wasn't sure which was scarier.

"Okay, one more rule," Kerri said.

"What is this, some kind of power trip?" I asked.

"Shh! This one is important," Kerri said. "You are no longer to think about, memorize the schedule of and attempt to bump into, or try in any other way to communicate with one Josh Marx."

"Kerri—"

"I'm serious here, Quinn," she said. "This entire plan

will go south if you keep making your cute but totally misguided and ineffective attempts to get his attention. You need to focus on this or it's never gonna work."

I took a deep breath and blew it out dramatically. She was right. I had to quash the idea of me and Josh for good.

"Fine," I said finally.

"Great! So this is it!" Kerri said, slapping her hands together. "One of these guys is the love of your life. Or at least a hot hook-up. Or a date to homecoming."

She clapped me once on the shoulder and stood up to get back to the all-important decision of what to wear to school. Meanwhile, I was practically melting into the floor. A hot hook-up? This was another area in which I had zero experience. Well, unless you count all those stupid seven-minutes-in-heaven experiments back in middle school and that time Doug Merickle grabbed me at the Holiday Ball after-party and drunkenly stuck his tongue down my throat. I had always sort of been saving myself for Josh. I wanted my first real kiss, my first everything, to be perfect. And I had always thought that he was the only perfect person out there.

The image of his tonsil-hockey match with Danielle flashed through my mind again. Screw Josh Marx. I was sick of listening to my friends talk about their hook-ups. I was sick of having *nada* to contribute. Of feeling like a naïve little goody-goody. It was time for Quinn Donohue to go out there and get some!

Oh, God. Nerves. Bile. I couldn't think about this anymore. I scooped up the three pictures and stuffed them into my pocket. One step at a time.

# three

Senior year. This was the supposed to be the year that I walked into Garden Hills High all confident, with my head held high knowing that I was the oldest, the coolest, the one nobody could mess with. Instead I was so tense that one loud noise would have sent me speeding for the hills. Thanks a lot, Kerri.

I navigated the front hall packed with confused, giggly freshmen and the upperclass boys who were checking them out. I found Kerri waiting at my locker.

"Hey," I said, starting in on my combination.

"Hey."

There was a moment of silence as I opened my locker and tossed my lunch inside.

"Quinn! Aren't you going to say anything?" she asked.

I glanced at her. She executed a little spin. Oh, right. The outfit. She'd gone with a pair of skinny jeans and a red top with a neckline so wide it fell off one shoulder.

"Oh, yeah. Sorry. Good choice," I said flatly.

I myself had gone with my most broken-in tan cargo pants, a vintage black AC/DC T-shirt, and my yellow Chuck D's. My hair was back in a ponytail, and, as always, I wore my leather cuff bracelet on one arm and my grandfather's silver watch on the other.

"Thanks. Very enthusiastic," she said, leaning back against the lockers.

"I'm sorry, all right? I'm just nervous." I slammed my locker as hard as I could. Unfortunately it didn't make me feel any better.

"Oh, right!" Kerri's eyes lit up. "When are you going to ask out your first guy?"

I took a deep breath and rolled my shoulders back. "Today," I said. Wave of nausea. "I think I need to get it over with. Like ripping off a Band-Aid."

"Wow. I'm impressed," Kerri said, watching a pack of guys as they strode by us. "I fully thought you were going to wuss out."

"Ha," I said.

Wait a minute. Was that an option?

"So, which one are you going to ask first?" She pushed herself away from the lockers, and we started down the hallway toward the senior homerooms.

"All of them," I said with a nod.

Kerri stopped in her tracks. "*All* of them? Like, at once?

What're you, sending a mass e-mail or something?"

"No!" Actually, not a bad idea. But that really *would* be wussing out. "I barely slept last night, thinking about this. I just want to get it over with."

"Okay. I think you should go with Max first," she suggested.

"Logic, please?" I asked, turning the corner.

"Well, he's probably been asked out by *hundreds* of girls," Kerri answered. "He's used to it, so it won't be awkward or anything."

I paused in front of Mr. Julliard's homeroom, feeling even sicker than I had when I "woke up." (I wasn't sure I'd actually slept at all.)

"Huh. Why does knowing he's been asked out by *hundreds* of girls not make me feel better?" I said.

The bell rang, and Kerri eyed me sympathetically. "You'll be fine. I'll see you in gym!"

She scurried off down the hall, and I sighed. Yeah. I would be fine. Sure. I walked into homeroom, fell into one of the chairs near the back, and dropped my head onto my arms. Thirty seconds into day one, and I was already *so* over school.

*Come on, Quinn. You're doing this for a reason,* I told myself. *You're doing this to get over Josh Marx once and for all.*

I realized with a start that this was the first time I had thought about Josh all morning. Usually I spent the entire drive to school wondering if I would see him, whether he would say hello to me, and whether I would actually be

21

able to say hello back.

Huh. Seemed like Kerri's plan was already working.

First-day-of-school gym is a joke. They don't make you change or do anything sporty, so after they take attendance we always just end up sitting in the bleachers for fifty-five minutes, gossiping about what we did all summer. This year wasn't much different. Except for the topic of my and Kerri's conversation.

"He's right there," Kerri whispered, lifting her chin as Max and a few of his soccer buddies got up to kick a ball around in front of the bleachers. "Just do it."

"I'm going to start calling you 'Nike,'" I told her.

She shrugged and leaned back on her elbows. "I've been called worse. Come on. This is the one time you're going to get him when he's not surrounded by girls."

I took a deep breath. Max's deep eyes glinted in the sunlight streaming in from the high windows. He had dark longish hair and a great tan, as if he'd spent the entire summer at the beach, and he wore a light blue and white Hawaiian shirt over shorts. Basically he was a hot, Australian beach bum who could juggle a soccer ball for a hundred touches without its hitting the ground once. Why had I never noticed him before?

*Because of Josh*, a little voice told me. Josh, who was a few rows behind me on the bleachers, with Danielle DeLaurentis's freshly Nair-ed legs hooked over his own.

"All right," I said. "I'm going in."

I stood and wiped my palms on my thighs, then walked

shakily down the bleachers. *Eye on the ball,* a voice in my mind told me. *Swing through. Don't hesitate.*

I guess all my motivational phrases are about softball.

"Hey," I said to the guys on the gym floor. "Can I get in?"

Darren O'Donovan, star forward, backed up and kicked the ball to me. I juggled it a couple times, then popped it to Mike Tafono. Mike did a cool behind-the-back kick and tossed it to Max, who went foot to knee to foot again. As we went around the circle one more time, my mouth started to go dry. This was torture. What was I going to do? Ask him out right in front of Darren and Mike? Not likely. I had to get him away from them. And to do that, I had only one choice.

When the ball came my way again, I went against every fiber of my naturally competitive being and screwed up on purpose. I let the ball fly off the top of my foot, booting it halfway across the gym—right over Max's head.

"Nice one," Darren joked.

"I got it," Max said, turning to chase after it.

Huh. Maybe I *was* good at this.

I chased after the ball as well, and all of a sudden the two of us were half a basketball court away from everyone else. We reached for the ball at the same time, but Max picked it up.

"Hey," he said, seeming surprised to see me there. "You're pretty good."

He had the coolest accent. Like Russell Crowe or Heath Ledger.

"Thanks. You, too," I said honestly. I could talk about

sports skills all day. But sadly that wasn't what I was here for.

I looked at Kerri. She stared back at me. My underarms prickled with sweat. My breath was so shallow, I was sure I was going to faint. Inside my head my little voice was shouting at me. *Do it! Do it now! Now, now, NOW!*

"Would you want to go out with me sometime?" I blurted. At his back. He was already walking away. Instantly all conversation in the bleachers halted. I guess I had spoken a little too loudly. I saw Josh Marx watching me. Danielle laughed.

*Kill me. Just kill me now.*

Slowly Max turned around. He looked at me quizzically. "Really?"

*Seriously. Dead. Now. Me. Fine.*

"Uh . . . I . . ."

*Very good at sentence forming, I am.*

"Sure," he said with a smile.

All the air rushed back into my lungs. *What? Sure? Did he really just say* sure?

"Remember this number," he said, tossing the soccer ball back and forth from one hand to the other. As if this wasn't a life-altering moment happening right now. "Five-five-five; seven-eight-two-three."

"Five-five-five; seven-eight-two-three," I repeated. *555-7823. 555-7823.*

"Cool," he said. Then he winked and jogged back to his friends.

I caught Kerri's eye from across the room, and her grin

practically knocked me off my feet. *See? How easy was that?*

Okay. One down, two to go. I felt a little more confident as I walked out of the lunch line with my Snapple that afternoon. If I had asked out Max Eastwood, of all people, how hard could the others be? Of course, asking out Corey still felt too weird, so I decided Owen should be my next victim. But how do you ask out a person who never looks anyone in the eye?

I saw Owen settling his six-foot-four frame into one of the cafeteria chairs a few tables away. His dark hair was cut short at the sides and slightly longer on top. He had a light tan that brought out the freckles across his nose. He was wearing his varsity jacket over his T-shirt and jeans, even though it was still summer-hot out. Owen always wore his varsity jacket. I remember actually being confused when I saw him working the snack bar at The Mill back in June and realized it was because he wasn't covered in red and gold.

Already chowing down across from him was Drew Spencer—class wise-ass and Owen's best friend. These two were the oddest couple since Penn and Teller. Drew wore a backward baseball cap and an oversized T-shirt with what was undoubtedly some offensive graphic on the front. He'd been sent home for wardrobe violations even more often than Danielle DeLaurentis who usually came to school half-naked. I took a deep breath and headed over. Drew stopped talking when he saw me coming and watched me like a hawk as I sat down next to them. Owen merely glanced in my direction, turned blotchy, and returned his attention to his hamburger.

"Lose your map or somethin', sweetheart?" Drew asked loudly.

Now it was my turn to go blotchy.

"Drew," Owen said in a warning tone.

So he *did* speak.

"What? I'm just sayin'!" Drew exclaimed. "You're about eight tables off course."

He smirked as if he found my presence amusing. My heart pounded with humiliation. All right. Clearly this was a mistake. I stood up.

"Wait," Owen said.

Drew looked about as startled as I was. Owen cast a shy glance in my general direction.

"Did you want something?" he asked.

It seemed like it had taken him a lot of effort to find these words. This was ridiculous. He might be the one person on the planet who was shyer than I was. I was supposed to ask him out? I looked across the room to the table where Kerri and a few of our friends sat. Kerri gave me an encouraging, wide-eyed "Nike" look. At that moment I just wanted to smack her upside the head. What was she thinking?

"I . . . uh . . . wanted to see if maybe you wanted to go out sometime," I mumbled quickly, feeling miserable. Even my shoulders sagged.

Owen turned fully scarlet. Drew's jaw dropped as if it were made of lead. *Just say no so we can get this over with,*

I thought desperately.

"You like my boy?" Drew exclaimed, executing a deft attitude shift. "How about that?"

"Drew!" Owen said through clenched teeth.

I stood there, feeling as if I had a huge bull's-eye on my chest with the word *loser* painted across it. People at neighboring tables were starting to take notice. Finally, *finally,* Owen huffed out a breath and turned to me. He actually looked right at me. His eyes were this light, clear blue like nothing I had ever seen before.

"Seriously?" he said.

Why did no one seem to believe me when I asked them out?

"Yeah," I replied.

Owen looked somewhere past my left shoulder as he seemed to mull this over. I swear it had taken the Iraqi government less time to decide on a constitution.

"Okay. Yeah," he said finally. "Should I . . . what? Call you or something?"

His eyes met mine again for a split second. I glanced away. "Yeah. That's cool. My number's in the student directory."

"Okay," Owen said firmly, still looking a bit confused.

"Okay," I repeated. Then I turned and hightailed it over to my regular table, ignoring the sounds of Drew hooting and hollering as if Owen had just won on *The Price Is Right*.

That evening, after the heat started to wane a little, I headed over to the skate park. I gotta say, I was feeling kind of good about myself. Kerri had gushed for about an hour over the fact that I had managed to land two dates before sixth period. And she was right. I mean, Max Eastwood and Owen Meyer were two of the most gorgeous guys in school. Who gave a crap about Josh Marx? Apparently I *was* a hottie!

Ha.

I took a few runs on the big ramp and got my blood pumping. Soon my heart was pounding and I had a nice line of sweat across my forehead. I smiled as I picked up speed and executed a smooth 360 at the top of the ramp. This was a good day.

I popped up on the other side of the ramp and sat down on the edge, my legs crooked over the side and my elbows propped behind me on my board. Off to the west the sun was sinking toward the horizon, bathing the sky in pinks and yellows. A light breeze cooled my skin. This was my favorite time of day. I felt relaxed. Chill. Totally in control.

Then I saw Corey board up, and my heart went spastic on me. I should have known he would be here.

"Yo, Donny!" he shouted as he climbed the steps behind the ramp.

"Hey," I replied. My voice sounded strained.

Corey dropped down next to me and handed me a Snapple Raspberry Iced Tea. "You just get here?" he asked, popping open his own bottle.

"Been here a while," I told him. I set my drink aside. Sugar was definitely not what I needed.

"I had a student council meeting after school," he said.

"The reps are a bunch of tools this year. Guess I'll just have to take charge, right?" he added with a grin.

I looked at him and tried to see past the Corey I knew, looking for the Corey I could possibly date. Everyone knew the kid was hot. His mom was white and his dad was African-American, which had resulted in pretty much the greatest gene-splice ever. He was tall and broad with dark hair, light skin, and these amazing green eyes. Plus he had that politician's smile. He could charm the pants off anyone, from students to teachers to janitors.

Corey was also a prep. He was sitting there in a rugby shirt and khaki shorts. Not your stereotypical boarder. He caught a lot of smack from the other guys at the skate park for his style—until they saw him board.

"So, whaddup, D?" he asked, lifting his bottle to his lips. "Great sunset, huh?"

"Would you ever want to go out on a date with me?" I blurted out point-blank.

Half his Snapple came out his nose. He slapped his free hand to his face and made a few convulsive choking sounds.

"Are you okay?" I asked nervously.

"I'm fine! Fine." He coughed. He wiped his mouth with the back of his hand and looked at me. "What?" he said. "I mean, I . . . what?"

This time I was prepared for the shock. I mean, *I* was shocked I was asking him. "Look. You haven't been out on a date since Elena dumped you last year, right?"

Corey winced. "Harsh!" He paused and looked out over

the ramp, where a couple of guys were flying back and forth. "But true."

"Okay, and I haven't been on a date . . ."

"Ever?" Corey suggested.

My turn to wince. "Right. So why not just do it? See how it works out?"

Corey stared at me for a minute, as if he was trying to figure out if I was really insane or really smart. The longer he stared, the warmer I grew. Those eyes were incredible.

"Like a practice run," he said. "Like getting back on the horse. Or, for you, getting on the horse for the first time."

I scrunched my nose in disgust. "Can we kill the horse analogy?"

Corey laughed. "You know what, Donny? I'm in. Why not?"

I couldn't have been more relieved. It was over. I had done it. I had asked out all three guys, and, miraculously, they had all said *yes*.

"Cool," I said.

I opened my Snapple, took a long drink, then got up and jumped onto my board. Maybe Kerri wasn't insane after all. Not that I'd ever tell her that.

# four

"Do you really not own one skirt?" Kerri shouted from inside my walk-in closet that Friday night. She had to shout—next door my little brother, Jack, was listening to his latest hard rock obsession at full volume. He was thirteen years old with a birthday coming up, and I swear he was trying to deafen us all before he hit the big one-four.

"Okay, I'm starting to think you *really* don't know me," I called back.

I flopped down on my unmade bed, which was covered with the piles of clothes Kerri had brought over for my date with Max—all of which I had rejected. I felt ill. Majorly ill. I wanted to be excited about this date. I really did. But it's tough to get excited about something when you feel like you're about to hurl every five seconds. What if Max didn't like me? What if he turned out to be a jerk? What were we going to talk about? What if he tried to kiss me? I was totally inexperienced, and he had kissed, what, dozens of girls? What if I messed it up?

My head was resting on something sharp. I whipped out a studded belt and flung it to the floor, then rested my hands against my swirling stomach.

"Do you have any idea what I would do for a closet this size?" Kerri asked, stepping to the door. She pulled one of my helmets out from behind her back. "And all you've got in here is skateboard crap."

"Hey, that helmet is state-of-the-art," I told her, lifting my head only slightly.

Kerri sighed like she was talking to a kindergartner. A slow one. "Are you *sure* you don't want to wear something of mine?"

"What about the whole 'just be you' thing?"

"You can be you in a skirt," she said.

"No. I can't," I replied. "I fidget when I wear skirts. And this?" I sat up and grabbed a high-heeled shoe from the floor. "This might kill me. I'm wearing something of my own."

Kerri narrowed her eyes at me. "So, if it's in this closet, you'll wear it?"

"If it's in that closet, I'll wear it," I replied confidently.

"I am *so* going to find something."

I scoffed. "Good luck."

As she rummaged through my jeans and boots and Converses and Windbreakers, I sighed and looked around my room, sort of wishing I was just hanging in its cozy confines for the night. I wondered if any one of these guys would still agree to go out with me if they caught a glimpse of the insanity I lived in. One morning last summer I had woken up and suddenly hated with poisonous intensity the yellow walls I'd had since birth. I went to Home Depot, bought two gallons of black paint, and painted the whole thing in one day. Then I realized how depressing it was and covered almost every last inch of wall with posters of bands, boarders, softball players, and Orlando Hernandez, my favorite baseball pitcher. It was eclectic—and beyond messy—but it was home.

"Aha!"

That didn't sound good. Had the fashion fairy dropped a pink, pleated, Hilton miniskirt in my closet overnight?

"Aha, what?"

"I found something!" she singsonged.

"You found nothing," I replied.

"Oh, yes, I did." She popped out of my closet with an above-the-knee sundress that was covered in little blue flowers. My stomach turned. How could I have forgotten that was in there?

"*Where* did this come from?" Kerri asked, holding it up in front of herself in the mirror.

"I don't even know," I said with a groan. "My mom bought it and made me wear it to my grandfather's birthday party last summer."

Kerri grinned slowly. "Well . . . it was in your closet!" she sang out.

"Kerri—"

"Quinn, look. You are going out with one of the most coveted guys in our class," Kerri said. "You think any of the other girls he's dated have shown up in cutoffs and flip-flops? Put some effort in already."

I looked her up and down. She was already dressed for Kyle Stoller's party—the first big bash of the year—and she looked incredible. Like worthy-of-going-out-with-Max-Eastwood incredible. Maybe I should take her fashion advice. Just this once.

I slumped down on the bed. "Can I at least wear my Birks with it?"

"Can I look now?" I asked as Kerri leaned toward my face and studied her work. I felt like someone had smeared my skin with peanut butter and then poked me in the eyes several times. Actually, the second part was pretty much true.

Mercifully Jack had cut the music and gone downstairs to play video games before the jabbing and stabbing and rubbing had started. If he hadn't, I'd probably have a migraine by now.

"Not yet," she said. "Close."

"What is this, the dentist?" I asked.

"Just close your eyes," she said patiently.

I did. She drew on them some more. I flinched. She sighed. It was getting really old.

"Okay. Open," she said. My vision was a little blurred, but I could see she was smiling. "You're done!"

I turned around and looked into the mirror. My eyes widened, which was a little surreal, considering they already looked the size of baseballs. My lashes were curled, my eyes were outlined in black, my cheeks were flushed, and my lips were so red, I might have just been punched. At least she'd kept my ponytail, but only because the rubber band had left a dent in my otherwise stick-straight hair when she tried to take it out.

"I'm a hooker," I said.

"No, you're not! This is the absolute minimum I would wear for a date. I swear," Kerri said.

"Oh," I said, blinking at her. "So *you're* a hooker."

"Ha-ha," she said, throwing her tools of torture back into her case, a purple version of my father's tackle box. "It only looks like too much because you never wear any."

"I'm washing it off," I said, standing up.

"No, you're not," she replied. Just as she grabbed for my arm, the doorbell rang.

My body felt like a bolt of electricity had shot straight through it. I swear I almost peed in my pants as every fiber of my being trembled.

"He's here!" Kerri said excitedly. "You don't have time to wash it off."

I was going to kill her. I really was. She was sending me out looking like Ronald Mc-freakin'-Donald. In a dress!

"Oh, my God, Kerri. What am I going to do? What am I going to say? What are we going to talk about?" I cried, flipping into panic mode.

"First you are just going to go down there and say

hello," she replied calmly. "After that, you'll wing it."

I took a deep breath and nodded. Downstairs I could hear my mother greeting Max. Max Eastwood was in my house right now. For me.

"Quinn! Max is here!" my mother called up the stairs.

"This is going to be great," Kerri told me, laying her hands on my shoulders. My *bare* shoulders. "You are going to have so much fun."

"Right. Yeah. You think?" I said.

She turned me around and basically shoved me toward the door. My knees felt like Jell-O as I walked down the stairs to the foyer. Max was chatting casually with my mom, as if he chatted with moms all the time. He wore baggy shorts and a short-sleeved white surf shirt open at the collar, which brought out his tan. He looked, in a word, *yum*.

"Here she is," my mother said with an embarrassingly large smile. She'd been ridiculously excited to hear I had a date. Her eyes lit up when she saw me. "Quinn! You're wearing the—"

"Mom!" I said through gritted teeth.

She pressed her lips together. The benefit of having a youngish mom is that she remembers vividly what it felt like to be humiliated by her own mother. Thank goodness my dad was working late. He wasn't down with the self-restraint.

"Wow," Max said. "You look . . ." He glanced at my mother. "Beautiful."

Suddenly my heart was all aflutter. I had a feeling that

before he'd remembered my mom was there, he was about to say *hot*. Either one was fine by me. Kerri was officially forgiven.

"Hope you don't mind coming here," Max said to me an hour later. "There's not much to choose from in this town."

"Are you kidding? It's fine," I said.

We were sitting at a table at Tino's Pizza, the hole-in-the-wall that kids from school go to after every game and late-night rager. The wallpaper is a hideous print of red grapes and guys on donkeys. The black marble counter is cracked in five places. Tino himself gives off these noxious fumes that make you wonder if he bathes in his own garlic sauce. But honestly, where else was there in Garden Hills for him to take me? We had the distinction of living in one of the most boring of all the boring Baltimore suburbs. It was either here, the Burger King, or the Dairy Queen. There was only one nice restaurant in town—The Terrace—and it was total adult territory, the place where our parents went on their anniversaries or to celebrate Valentine's Day. When it came to dating, everyone in my school had low expectations. Tino's was a number-one first date venue.

And still, even with the less than romantic surroundings, all I could think about as I munched on my pepperoni slice was crawling across the rickety table and jumping Max.

I know. Somewhere between the makeup and the menu I had lost my mind.

In my defense, Max was completely and totally

gorgeous. It was as if he had a spotlight fixed on him at all times, making his dark hair shine and his tan skin glow. His smile was relaxed and confident and put me completely at ease. But it also stirred things inside of me that should not be stirred while I was trying to eat. I didn't even fidget with my dress. I was too busy staring at the line of his chest muscle that appeared just above the top button of his shirt every time he leaned forward. How was it possible that I had never noticed this guy before?

Oh, yeah. Because I'd been obsessed with Josh Marx.

"So, I was thinking that after this we could hit Kyle Stoller's party," Max said, leaning back in his chair.

"Oh. Okay." I was both disappointed and psyched by this suggestion. Disappointed because: a) it meant that he wasn't salivating to be alone with me, and, b) I wasn't a big fan of monster bashes and all the drinking and puking and debauchery that went on. Psyched because: a) it meant that I wouldn't have to stress about being alone with him some-where and dealing with this full-on lust thing, and, b) well, actually, that was pretty much it.

"So, you're in charge of homecoming and the Spirit Show skit, right?" he asked.

I loved his accent. Love, love, *loved* it. It made me think of huge white beaches and crashing waves and Max walk-ing around all shirtless and sunkissed. So sexy.

"Yeah. Me and Corey," I told him, taking a sip of my Coke.

"How did you get into that?" he asked. "Forgive me, but when I think of homecoming, I think of the cheerleading squad. And you are no cheerleader."

Something about the way he looked at me when he said that made me think he liked that I was not a rah-rah.

I snorted an uncomfortable but flattered laugh. "No. I'm not. Actually I was never into school spirit and all that, but a couple years ago I realized that the Spirit Club was decorating the guys' basketball and baseball teams' lockers before every game, but no one so much as acknowledged the girls' basketball team or our softball games, so my friend Kerri and I joined up and got it started."

*Wow. Nice run-on sentence there, Quinn.*

Max grinned. "So, you're a revolutionary."

I blushed. "I don't know about that."

A silence fell, and I picked up my soda and drained it just to give me something to do. The second I placed the empty cup down on the table, Max snapped his fingers at the greasy waiter and ordered me another.

"So . . . uh . . . what about you? How did you get started in soccer?" I asked.

He sat up and leaned his elbows on the table. Up close I noticed his lips were shiny—from pizza grease or saliva, I had no idea—and I couldn't stop staring at them.

"My mother plays," he said. "She signed me up for a team when I was four. She grew up here, in the U.S., but she married my dad in Australia, and they stayed there. I'm living with her sister now, my aunt."

"Is it hard? Being away from your family?" I asked, tearing my eyes away from his mouth. My heart pounded as he met my gaze directly.

"It is. I miss my brothers mostly," he said. "But they're proud of me, that I'm doing so well here. And I can get a good education at an American college."

The waiter placed my soda down in front of me, but I couldn't look away from Max long enough to even say thank you. How could someone my own age be this sure of himself? It was fascinating to me.

"So, Quinn, what are your favorite bands? Your favorite movies?" he asked suddenly.

I laughed at the directness of the question. "Why?"

"Because I want to get to know you," he said with a shrug.

My heart warmed and I sipped my soda. If this was what all dates were like, I had seriously been missing out.

Kyle Stoller lives in one of the biggest houses in town, and it was already overflowing with people when we arrived. Kyle throws all of Garden Hills' big ragers because: a) his parents travel a lot, b) he has a tremendous need to be popular, and c) he lives up on this huge hill at the top of this ridiculous winding road, and it takes the ten or so town cops at least half an hour longer to get there than it would take them to get anywhere else, thereby giving the student population that much longer to get drunk and act stupid.

Not that I really care. I'd just rather spend the night listening to downloads in my garage and airbrushing a new board. Still, instead of being prematurely irritated, the way I usually was when Kerri dragged me to these things, I was kind of excited as Max and I slipped by the kids milling outside the front door. I guess Max was having a positive effect on me.

The second we walked through the door, a couple of junior guys came barreling down the stairs, chasing each other with massive water guns. I jumped back, Max jumped forward, and the guys raced right between us, almost knocking me over. Max shot them a scathing look as they ran off, taking down a large vase full of fake flowers in the process.

"You okay?" he asked me, his brow furrowed.

"Yeah. I'm fine."

"Here," he said. And then he took my hand. He *took* my *hand*. I couldn't stop grinning as Max navigated his way into Kyle's massive living room, weaving through the crowd and slapping his friends' palms. No one had ever held my hand before. Except my dad. And then I was, like, eight.

"Hi, Max!" Grace Ricardo, one of the Glossies, called out. She practically bowled over half the people in her way trying to get to Max. Then her eyes fell on our entwined fingers. Her expression dropped, then quickly recovered. "Hi, Quinn," she said.

"Hey," I replied.

Then she dove back into the crowd, undoubtedly to share the news of my hand-holding with all her little Glossy friends. They would probably have a group coronary, then drown their confusion in low-carb wine coolers for the rest of the night.

See, guys like Max date girls like Grace. They don't date

girls like me. Well, until now.

Max paused at the back of the room and stood on tip-toe. "Looks like there's a huge line at the bar," he said. "Want to stay here, and I'll get us something?"

"Sure," I said, feeling semi-giddy.

"I'll be right back," he assured me.

I leaned against a wall in my daze and watched him go—me and the rest of the party's female population. Everyone wanted him, but he was coming back to me. Me! I'd be lying if I said it didn't feel good.

I usually thought it was totally lame and predictable when people coupled off at these things and went off looking for an empty bedroom, but just about then it was all I wanted to do. Of course I had no idea what I'd do when I got there, but I was definitely willing to let Max help me figure it out.

"Hey, Quinn."

Instant goose bumps popped up all over my arms. I knew that voice.

"Hey," I managed to say as I turned to face Josh. He was holding a beer in one hand, and he leaned casually against the wall next to me as if this was an everyday thing. He was wearing a heather-gray T-shirt that brought out his eyes and he looked *F-I-N-E*. My already racing heart went into spastic overdrive.

*No*, I told myself. *No Josh. You are attracted to Max now*. Could a girl be this attracted to two guys at the same time? It hardly seemed healthy.

Josh looked me up and down, and I waited for him to

comment on the dress or the makeup. Anyone who knew me even the slightest bit would have been surprised. But instead he nodded toward the bar area and said, "Did I just see you walk in with Max Eastwood?"

A hot flush raced all the way up my body from my toes to my temples. For a person who'd never seemed to care that I existed, this was an intriguing question. First of all, he had *noticed* us, which was beyond cool. But why did he care? Was he jealous all of a sudden? Seriously?!

"Yeah," I said, trying to play it cool. "So?"

"Nothing," he said, shrugging one shoulder. "I just never would've put you two together."

What the hell did *that* mean?

"Yeah, well, I never would have put you and Danielle DeLaurentis together," I shot back.

"That's over, anyway," he said, then took a sip of his beer.

The reaction in my stomach was near psychotic, but I didn't have a chance to follow up, because at that moment Max returned with two cups of punch.

"Hey, man," Max said, lifting his chin.

"Hey," Josh replied. He stood up straight, and before I knew it, they were both standing there with their shoulders squared, sort of sizing each other up. Toe-to-toe. Testosterone everywhere. It would have been hilarious if I wasn't right in the center of it feeling totally confused.

"Mind if I talk to my date?" Max said finally.

Josh shrugged. "Sure."

The moment he was gone, my body temperature finally returned to normal, and I collapsed back against the wall.

"Was he bothering you?" Max asked, handing me the punch.

I laughed. I couldn't help it. This was too bizarre. All I had wanted for five years was for Josh Marx to talk to me, and now I had Max Eastwood protecting me from just that. "Uh, no."

"Because I'll talk to him if he was," Max said.

I looked at him, trying to figure out if he was serious. He was. Kind of archaic, right? But sweet, I guess. "It's okay," I told him. "I can take care of myself."

Max moved closer to me, and all my senses went on alert. "I just don't want anyone interrupting our date," he whispered.

Suddenly I found myself staring at his lips again. They were right there, at eye level, and all I could think about was how soft they looked. I bit my bottom lip just to keep from licking it. Max looked down at me. His arm slid around my back and I felt the warmth of his leg against mine.

Oh. My. God.

"Wanna go somewhere?" he asked. He took both our drinks and placed them on a bookcase nearby.

"Like where?" I heard myself say.

Max glanced around, grabbed my hand, and led me back through the party. I was so overwhelmed with excitement and giddy anticipation, I could barely see straight. What was I doing? This was so not me. But that was exactly what made me want to do it even more.

He stepped into the family room where a few people were hanging out, talking loudly over some random action movie on the TV. Max glanced around, and yanked open the door to a closet. Just then I spotted Kerri staring at me from across the room. She had a wide-eyed look that was both shocked and psyched. The girl knew exactly what Max had in mind.

*Oh, my God!* she mouthed to me as Max stepped into the closet, my hand still in his.

*I know!* I mouthed back.

I just caught a glimpse of her thumbs-up before Max pulled me in behind him.

I inhaled the sweet-musty scent of old cardboard boxes and dusty shelves. Light slanted in through a high window, and I could hear people outside milling around. Max closed the door quietly, and my heart seized up. Suddenly he was right there, inches from me, sliding his hands across my cheeks to cup my face.

He looked me in the eye, his expression intense. I couldn't breathe to save my life. And then, without a word, he kissed me.

I instantly lost all ability to stand and fell back against a shelf full of board games. Something was pressing into the small of my back, but I didn't care. Max's soft lips parted mine and our tongues found each other's slowly, almost carefully. This was nothing like Doug Merickle's sloppy, athletic, lizard-tongue acrobatics. This . . . *this* . . . was perfect.

Apparently Max either didn't know or didn't care that I was so inexperienced. Either that or he was determined to knock the innocence right out of me. The very idea made me giddy.

Slowly Max deepened the kiss, pressing his whole body against mine. Suddenly I became aware of the fact that I had arms and hands, and I wrapped myself around him, pulling him even closer. When he finally broke away, my vision was so blurred, I almost toppled over again.

"Wanna go back to the party?" he asked dazedly.

I just shook my head and pulled him to me again. *I can't believe I'm doing this. I can't believe I'm doing this.*

And then I giggled—yes, giggled—into his lips. I had a lot of lost time to make up for.

# five

By the time I sat down in the passenger seat of Owen's old Subaru on Saturday afternoon, I didn't see any reason for me to be there. I couldn't stop thinking about my night with Max, and every time I did, I shivered with pleasure. But I couldn't cancel with Owen—not after I had asked *him* out. That would be beyond rude, and even more awkward than asking him in the first place. Of course, ten minutes into the car ride, I was regretting my decision to be nice. So far neither one of us had said anything other than "Hey."

*Say something,* I urged myself. I was starting to sweat from the uncomfortable silence. *Just ask him something about . . . anything!*

I was kind of curious about why he had suggested an afternoon date, but I couldn't think of a way to ask him that without sounding disappointed and/or obnoxious. Instead I just looked out the window at the familiar tree-lined streets, the kids on their bikes, the ice-cream truck parked in the middle of Washington Park. Then he turned onto Old Mill Road and I finally snapped to. "We're going to The Mill?"

Owen nodded as he turned into the parking lot.

"I didn't bring a suit," I told him. Couldn't he have at least opened his mouth to give me special wardrobe requirements?

"Oh, I . . . we're . . . not going swimming," he stammered. "Unless you wanted to. We could go back. . . ."

He was getting all blotchy again.

"No. That's okay," I said, not wanting him to stress out more. "I don't need to swim."

Then what were we doing here?

Owen parked and got out of the car. He waited on his side for me to come around, then silently led me over the little footbridge in front of the entrance and past the "security" guys—all of whom were a year behind us in school and none of whom actually cared about keeping people out unless they were freshmen or other "losers" they could torture.

Which begged the question, why bring a girl to work? Wouldn't he want to avoid this place on his day off?

Owen took me over to the snack bar and opened the EMPLOYEES ONLY door. I hesitated for a split second before following him in behind the counter. Two girls from school stood at the window taking orders for hot dogs and ice cream. They both looked over their shoulders at us, exchanged a confused glance, then shrugged.

"Um . . . what're we doing here?" I asked as Owen walked to the back of the small kitchen. He paused in front of an old-fashioned, waist-high freezer with dozens of doors in the top.

"You like ice cream?" he asked. He looked hopeful and tense all at the same time, one hand on the freezer, the other curled into a fist at his side.

"Who doesn't?" I said.

Owen cracked a smile that lit up the entire room. It actually made my heart catch. Wow. He should do that more often.

"What do you want?" he asked. "I can make you anything."

Okay, this was pretty cute. He was so eager to please. He reminded me of my brother Jack back when he was little and used to play restaurant.

"Okay. I'll take something with tons of chocolate," I said, leaning back against a shelf filled with paper plates and Styrofoam cups.

Owen nodded and silently got to work. I watched him pile a plastic dish high with chocolate chocolate-chip ice cream, chocolate sauce, and chocolate sprinkles. Then he topped the whole thing off with whipped cream and M&Ms. By the time he handed it to me, I thought I was in love.

Just kidding.

He made himself a smaller concoction with coffee and

49

strawberry ice cream and then led me outside to the benches by the shuffleboard courts. On the way I saw Josh striding over to the snack bar, twirling his whistle around his index finger. God, he looked hot. And tan. And shirtless. He paused when he saw me following Owen and opened his mouth as if he was about to say something. I ducked my head and quickened my pace before he could get a word in.

Owen and I sat down on one of the benches. The shuffleboards were behind the snack bar, and it was a lot quieter back here, away from the masses. A pair of little girls were using the shuffleboard courts for hopscotch, but otherwise we were alone.

We sat in silence and ate our ice cream, but I wasn't as uncomfortable as I had been in the car. Clearly Owen had a hard time making conversation, and I knew what that was like. He was no Max, but he was sweet in his own way. I looked at his profile as he ate and wondered if kissing him would be anything like kissing Max, but there was no sizzle at all when I imagined it. I was guessing not.

"This is really good," I said finally. "Thanks."

"Good. I'm glad you like it. I wasn't really sure what to do. . . ." Owen said slowly, not exactly meeting my eyes. He didn't have Max's dating experience, that was for sure. This was good and bad. I mean, who knows what Max had done or hadn't done—what he expected and what he was used to. Owen was definitely more on my novice playing field.

"No. This is great. Really."

And that was it. That was all either one of us said until

we were done eating. I scraped the last bit of syrup up with my plastic spoon, let out a satiated sigh, then tossed my bowl into a garbage can next to the game room. I pushed my hands into the pockets of my denim shorts and turned to look at him. He looked back at me quizzically.

"So . . ." I said.

"So," he replied.

This was going nowhere.

"What do we do now?" he asked me.

I had no idea. I was kind of thinking that going home would be a good idea. I mean, he was nice and all. And cute, especially when he smiled. But we couldn't spend the whole afternoon like this, could we?

I glanced into the game room, where a couple of middle-school kids were playing Ping-Pong. Next to them was the same old air-hockey table I used to play on all the time when I was little.

"I forgot they had air-hockey here," I said. "I used to dominate at air-hockey."

Owen scoffed. "Bet you couldn't take me."

I felt the thrill of a challenge and grinned. "I'll take that bet."


"Yes! Score!" I shouted, raising my fists into the air.

The group of bathing suit–clad little girls on the left side of the table cheered as the boys on the other side tipped their heads back and groaned.

"No way! You were totally over the line!" Owen protested.

"I so was not!" I shot back.

Owen tossed his paddle down and threw up his hands jokingly. "I don't think I can date a cheater."

"I don't think I can date a sore loser," I told him, grinning.

He made a big show of rolling his eyes and picking up the paddle again. He wasn't really losing. We were tied one match to one, and he was up to game point in this third round. We were actually having fun. Lots of it. Owen and I definitely shared a serious jones for competition.

"Come on, man," one of the boys said, turning his baseball cap around on his head. "Put her away."

"You got it," Owen said.

"You are so going down," I told him, readying for the puck.

Owen leaned over the table, narrowed his eyes in concentration, and slammed the puck right into my goal. I tried to block it, but it was too fast. All the little boys went crazy, high-fiving and hugging Owen. I looked at my cheering section and shrugged an apology.

"Sorry, girls."

A curly-haired blonde shook her head. "They're going to torture us for the rest of the day."

Sure enough, the boys had started jumping up and down chanting, "Boys rule! Boys rule! Boys rule!"

I really don't miss middle school.

"Good game," Owen said. He walked around the table and reached his right hand out.

I shook it with a wry smile. "I'll get you next time."

Owen smiled that unbelievable smile and flushed. "No doubt."

"So I'll work at The Mill until it closes at the end of September, and then I go back to the supermarket until basketball season," Owen told me as we turned onto my street.

"Do you like working?" I asked.

He shrugged. "It's okay. I just don't want to be a burden to my mom. She already works two jobs, and she has my little brothers. If I want to go to college next year, I need to put money away now."

Once you broke the ice with Owen, the conversation really flowed. In the past half hour I had found out more about him than probably anyone, other than Drew, knew. He told me all about his brothers, William and Robert, and how much he loved taking care of them. In fact, that was why he had suggested we see each other in the afternoon— he was babysitting that night. He was hoping to get at least a partial basketball scholarship, but if not he was going to go to community college for two years, then try to get an academic scholarship to the University of Maryland. Between work, studying, and babysitting, he was totally focused on his family and his future. No wonder he'd never had much of a social life.

I wanted to ask him what had happened to his dad, but I didn't think I knew him well enough yet to pry.

He stopped his car in front of my house, and I realized with a start that the moment had come. The kiss-or-no-kiss moment. The sun was just starting to set, and I looked over at him. My heart began to pound. I really wanted him to kiss me. I couldn't believe it. In the last twenty-four hours I had thought more about hooking up than I had in the rest of my life combined. Had Max turned me into some kind of hormonal slut?

"So," he said.

"So . . ."

I looked at him encouragingly, trying my best to tell him with my eyes that if he tried to kiss me I would absolutely kiss him back. After last night I felt like I had some idea what I was doing. I'm pretty sure neither one of us was breathing. Oh, God. Here came the blotches.

"See you in school?" he said, avoiding eye contact.

My heart dropped. "Okay. Yeah," I said, fumbling for the door handle. "I'll, uh . . . thanks. For everything."

Owen simply nodded, and the awkwardness factor sky-rocketed. I finally managed to open the car door and stumble out onto the sidewalk. I felt mortified as I jogged inside and whipped out my cell phone. I speed-dialed Kerri.

"So? How was it?" she asked the second she picked up.

"He didn't kiss me," I grumbled, miserable. "I was trying to send him signals, but—"

"Sweetie, you are so not ready to send signals," Kerri said with a laugh.

"Hello? I'm dying over here!" I told her.

"What do you want?" she said. "You got some from Max last night. Which, by the way, I'm still impressed by. You want every guy to slobber all over you?"

I flopped onto the couch, where Jack was ripping some guy's head off in a video game. He cheered as blood spurted everywhere. "No. I guess not," I told Kerri, eyeing my brother in disgust.

"Quinn, we're talking about Owen Meyer here," Kerri said. "Potentially the only kid in school with less experience than you."

"Gee, thanks."

"Die! Die! Die!" my brother screeched.

"You need help," I told him, getting up again.

He just snickered.

"All I'm saying is, you might have to give him a little more time," Kerri said. "He's not the assault-you-in-the-closet type."

I headed for the kitchen, the knot in my stomach easing slightly. "You're right. You're right," I said. "Thanks, Ker."

"No problem," she replied. "You know, it's kind of cool talking to you about actual dates instead of imaginary ones." She laughed.

I rolled my eyes. Two dates down, one to go.

six

I popped my board up, whipped my helmet off, and jogged up the steps to the Garden View Diner, another regular hangout for GHHS students. Once again my stomach was having a field day, and I had to wonder what the heck I thought I was doing, cramming three dates into twenty-four hours. But at least meeting Corey tonight for dinner left my Sunday free to chill with my dad and watch the Ravens game—our weekly ritual in the fall. A girl needed at least one day to relax, right?

I opened the door and held my breath. I couldn't believe I was actually here for a date with Corey Haskell. This could either be really fun or really, *really* awkward.

My mouth dropped open when I saw Corey standing next to the back booth in khaki pants and a blue V-neck sweater. Mr. Preppy. He had somehow gotten one of those movie-theater velvet ropes and placed it in front of the booth. On the table was a red rose in a vase and candles. He waved and smiled.

I kind of guffawed. Corey grinned as I made my way over. He rolled my board under the table next to his own.

"What are you doing?" I asked him.

He shrugged. "Just figured I would do it up right. Since it's our first date and all."

My cheeks hurt from smiling. This was so Corey. He never did anything half-assed. Not even a get-back-on-the-horse date with a friend. He unhooked the velvet rope and stepped back so that I could slide into the booth.

"So, what's your pleasure?" he asked, handing me one of the huge leather menus that none of us ever actually looked at. "Burger and fries or chicken fingers and fries?"

"I think I'll go burger and fries," I said.

"Excellent choice," he said smoothly.

He summoned the waitress over and ordered, throwing in a black-and-white milk shake for me. My favorite. Meanwhile I flipped through the songs on our mini jukebox. (There was one at every booth.) I dug out some quarters and ordered up a few tunes. Black Eyed Peas for Corey. All-American Rejects for me.

"So, when do you want to hold the first committee meeting?" Corey asked, drumming his hands on the table.

"Next week, I guess. We should get started ASAP. We cannot let the juniors beat us again."

Every year, on the day before homecoming, each class

puts on a themed skit at the Spirit Show, then the whole school votes for the best one. The seniors always used to win no matter what, but for the past two years the class just behind ours has won. They won as freshmen *and* sophomores. Total suckage. This year the theme was the musical *Grease*, and as seniors we had first pick of the songs. Since we were the senior homecoming reps, Corey and I would be in charge of our skit.

"I hear that," Corey said. "Those little twits can kiss my ass. We're gonna blow them outta the water."

"Any ideas?" I asked.

"Not a one," Corey replied.

I laughed and slouched back in my seat. Considering how nervous I'd been ten minutes ago, I was feeling pretty comfortable now. This didn't feel like a date at all. I was just hanging out with Corey. But was that a good thing, or a bad thing? Maybe I should be taking this a little more seriously. I sat up straighter.

"So, if this was, like, a *real* date . . . what would you normally talk about?" I asked.

"Well, I—"

Corey's eyes flicked toward the door, and his whole face changed. I turned around and saw the evil ex herself sidling in with her boyfriend, Logan Arnott, trailing behind her. Elena Marlowe, as always, looked more like she was going clubbing than lounging at a diner. As I watched, she laughed at something Logan said and rested her hand on his chest.

Corey quickly returned his attention to me and cleared

his throat. "What would I normally talk about on a date?"

He reached over and took my right hand in both of his. My entire body overheated unexpectedly. Whoa.

"I'm honored you chose to be by my side tonight, baby," he said, putting on a smooth-jazz kind of voice. "A girl as fine as you could have any man, and the fact that you want to be with me—damn—I'm the luckiest playa alive."

He gazed into my eyes for a long moment, and I swear—even though I knew he was fully kidding—my heart stopped beating. Then I cracked up laughing. Corey grinned and took a sip of his water.

"It's a gift," he said.

"Yeah, from hell," I replied.

"All right. What about you? What would you talk about on a date?" he asked.

I smirked and pulled his hand toward me. "Baby, you are so lucky to be out with a girl like me tonight—"

"Very funny," he said, pulling his hand back. We both laughed.

The waitress placed our drinks down in front of us, and I stopped laughing long enough to take a sip of my shake. This was actually fun.

I saw Corey's eyes dart toward the door again and turned to look. Josh Marx walked in with a bunch of his football buddies. I felt my cheeks go pink. Good Lord, was this guy *everywhere*? Then Elena and Logan were ushered to a booth directly across the restaurant from Corey and me. Elena was all smiles until she noticed us. Then her expression went flat. Logan didn't notice anything. He was already busy with the jukebox.

I could feel the tension in the air. Was this about to become a scene? I really detested scenes. Suddenly my cell phone rang, and I practically jumped out of my seat. I grabbed it out of my jacket pocket and checked the caller ID. It was Max.

Okay, make me a little more tense, why don't you? I pressed the OFF button as hard as I could.

"You need to get that?" Corey asked.

"No," I said, shoving it back into my pocket.

Then Josh and his friends crowded into the booth right behind Elena and Logan. Was it just me, or did Josh keep glancing our way? For a guy who saw right through me until earlier this summer, he sure seemed to be paying a lot of attention lately.

Corey raised his chin in their direction by way of hello.

Sometimes it sucks that Corey knows *everyone*. Josh took it as an invitation to come over.

"Hey, man." He slapped hands with Corey.

"Triple Threat!" Corey said.

I have no idea why he calls Josh that.

"So . . ." Josh said. "Big date?"

I guess he noticed the candles and the rose. And, oh, yeah, the big velvet rope.

I glanced up. "Yeah, kind of."

Josh's eyes widened, and he sort of frowned, as if he were considering this. Like he was surprised. Why did he seem to find it so shocking whenever he saw me with a guy?

"Well, then, I'll leave you to it," Josh said.

Oookay.

Josh walked back across the room, but he stopped at Elena and Logan's table on his way. Elena shot us an alarmed look, then asked Josh something. I tried not to stare, but I was too nervous about the potential drama. I wanted to see it coming if and when it came. Corey, however, casually toyed with his straw wrapper as if nothing was going on.

Finally Josh sat down with his friends, and seconds later Elena got up. My heart pretty much stopped. But instead of stalking over to us, she dragged Logan from his seat and out the front door. From the look of confusion on his face he still had no clue what was going on around him.

I sighed in relief when they were finally gone and our food arrived—perfect timing. The waitress placed our burgers down in front of us.

Corey, all grins, shot a look at the door, still closing behind his ex, and took a big bite of his burger. "This is fun," he said. "We should do it again sometime."

Once all the drama had passed, Corey and I talked about skateboarding and homecoming and college stuff. It was totally chill and fun and all in all a perfect way to spend a Saturday night. I never once wished I was back home with my airbrush and my MP3s. We boarded back through the quaint streets of Garden Hills together and stopped at the front walk to my house.

"You know what? You're not a bad date," Corey said.

"Thanks. I think," I replied with a laugh.

"No. I'm serious," he said. "I had fun."

"Me, too."

I looked at the sidewalk and pushed my board back and forth with the toe of one shoe. Here I was for the second time today. The Big Kiss moment. This was becoming a habit for me all of a sudden. But now it was Corey. He'd seen me biff face-first on the baby ramp. He was there last year when I puked after the Spirit Club pancake breakfast. Was he really going to want to go for the lips?

"Now, normally on a date, I would kiss the girl good night," Corey said.

My heart zinged heat in a zillion directions. I looked up and lifted one shoulder casually. "You gotta do what you gotta do."

Corey grinned. He leaned in close to me, hesitating for an agonizing second. I thought he was going to change his mind and run, but then he looked me in the eyes. Honestly, that one split second of eye contact was just as heart-catching as half an hour in the closet with Max. The anticipation was that good. Then he leaned in the rest of the way and touched his lips to mine.

This time I was more prepared than I had been with Max. At first the kiss was soft and timid. Then I opened my mouth slightly, and I felt Corey flinch. My heart swooped, and I opened my eyes, but I saw he was smiling. Instead of pulling back he wrapped his arms around me and pulled me in close, kissing me deeply. Everything inside me pounded.

I was kissing Corey Haskell. Corey Haskell was kissing

me. And I didn't want him to stop. If possible, it was even more perfect than kissing Max.

Whoa. Who knew?

Corey grinned like a moron when he finally pulled away. I think I did, too. My mind was totally fuzzy and soft and all I wanted to do was grab him and pull him back, but I was still too stunned that it had happened at all. He was my friend. One of my *best* friends. Was this just too weird? My humming lips didn't seem to think so.

"See ya on Monday?" he said.

"Yeah," I replied.

Then he boarded off toward his house a couple of blocks away. Considering how kinetic I was feeling, I don't know how he had the stability to ride. I kept waiting for him to fall over, but he made it around the corner without a hitch.

Grinning, I turned around and practically skipped into the house.

"I'm home!" I shouted.

"Have fun?" my mom and dad called back in unison from the kitchen.

"Yeah! I'll be there in a sec!"

I slammed the door, yanked out my cell phone, and turned it on. There was a message from Max. I listened to it, breathless, as I climbed the stairs to my room.

"Hi, Quinn. It's me, Max. Just wanted you to know I've been thinking about you all day. Call me back when you get a chance."

A lump caught in my throat. Thinking about me all day? Wow.

I dropped down at my desk and checked my e-mail. Three from Kerri and one from Owen. I had to laugh. Suddenly there were guys everywhere! I clicked on Owen's message.

Quinn-
Just wanted to say hey. Hope you had fun today.
I did. Gotta go. William's trying to melt Play-Doh
on the stove.
Owen

Aw, he was cute. My brain was all over the place. I flipped my phone open and called Kerri.

"Hey! How was the date?" she asked, shouting to be heard over a ton of background noise.

"Amazing," I said. "Where are you?"

"I just got out of the movies with Janice and Lindsey," she said. "So, spill."

Janice and Lindsey were the two friends from softball who we hung out with most often. They were as inseparable from each other as Kerri and I were.

"Yeah! How was the date with Corey?" I heard Lindsey ask in a suggestive voice.

"Kerri! Did you *tell* them about the three-man-plan?" I demanded.

"Sorry, I couldn't help it," she said. "It was such good dish."

I rolled my eyes, but let it go. Janice and Lindsey would have realized something was up sooner or later. Especially if I actually did start dating one of these guys. I just hoped they would keep their commentary to a minimum. Between Lindsey's bubbly take on life and Janice's more sarcastic, acerbic one, I had a feeling their advice would just confuse me more.

"So are you gonna tell me or not?" Kerri asked. "We're dying over here."

"Fine," I said. "It was great, Ker. So much fun and so chill, I guess because we already knew each other. And—get this—he kissed me."

"No!"

"Yes! Like *really* kissed me. And it was . . . God! It was unbelievable," I said, biting my lip.

"Damn, girl."

"I know!" I said, leaning back in my chair.

"What? What?" Lindsey and Janice chorused.

"He kissed her," Kerri told them quickly.

"Omigosh!" Lindsey gasped.

"Of course he did. He's a guy," Janice said flatly.

I laughed. Typical.

"Now *shhh*. I'm trying to talk. So this is good," she said to me.

"I know. But then I get home to an e-mail from Owen and a killer message from Max that I will have to play for you later."

"*Real*-ly?" she said suggestively.

I laughed again. "Kerri, I like them all. How did this happen? I don't know what the hell to do!"

"Uh, love every minute of it?" she suggested. "You have

three hot guys who want to jump you!"

Lindsey squealed in the background.

"I don't know about *that*," I said, flushing.

"Well, whatever, you don't have to decide tonight," she said. "Just . . . I don't know . . . sleep on it. You'll figure it out."

I sighed and stared at the e-mail, my lips still buzzing from Corey's kiss and my heart still pounding from Max's message. I hoped Kerri was right, because as of right now I was one confused chick.

seven

"So, when last we spoke yesterday, you had yet to make any major, life-altering decisions," Kerri said on Monday morning. I was waiting for her at her locker, so that I could wring her neck. "Any breakthroughs?"

"Only that I want a time machine and a new best friend," I grumbled.

"Excuse me?" she said with wide eyes. "Have you not just been on the three best dates of your life thanks to me? Wait! Revise. The *only* three dates of your life?"

"Yeah, great. And now I have insomnia, my mind won't stop racing, and I think I might be getting an ulcer," I said, even as the acid in my stomach flowed.

"Okay, calm down," Kerri said, popping open her locker. "Look, you're going to be fine. Sooner or later something's going to happen to make everything clear."

"Great. Now you're a fortune cookie," I said, leaning back against the locker next to hers. The cool steel felt lovely against my overheated skin. It had a calming effect. I wanted to stay there all day.

"Maybe one of them will back off. They can't *all* want you forever," Kerri said.

"Gee, thanks," I replied.

"You gotta admit, that would make it easier," she told me. Then something caught her eye over my shoulder. "Hey. Check it out."

I followed her discreet head tilt and saw Corey standing at his locker down the hall, engaged in a heated conversation with Elena. Instantly my already nuclear body-heat index popped the thermometer. Corey was all tense and rigid, but Elena kept advancing on him—touching his collar and his shoulder, shaking her curls back, tilting her chin down so she could look up at him through her lashes. Not good. Not good at all.

*Back off, bitch!* a voice in my head cried. Whoa. Was that *me*? I really needed some sleep.

"So typical," Kerri said, yanking textbooks out of her locker as she shook her head. "The second she sees him with another girl, she wants him back."

My mouth went dry. Not that I wasn't already thinking this. It just sucked to hear it from someone else. "You think?"

Suddenly I felt his kiss all over again, and it was making me ill. If he went back to Elena, I was going to feel like such an idiot.

Kerri slammed her locker and looked at me. "Wow. You're really not happy about this," she said, sounding surprised.

I blinked. *Get a grip.* "Nah! I'm fine!" I replied, shrugging. "It's just Corey, right? He can talk to whoever he wants."

"Oh, hey. Bachelor number two," Kerri said, ending that topic for the moment.

Sure enough, Owen was approaching uncertainly. He wiped a palm on his jeans, then shoved it into a pocket of his varsity jacket. He glanced at Kerri as if she might spontaneously combust at any moment, then looked me in the eye. The blotches were slowly forming.

"Uh . . . hey," he said. He looked at the ground.

"Hey, Owen," I replied.

He glanced at Kerri again, then at me. Someone grazed him on their way down the hall, and it nearly knocked him off balance. This was taking him a lot of effort.

"I . . . uh . . . I just wanted to say I had a really nice time on Saturday," Owen said, directing most of the sentence at the toes of his New Balance sneakers.

"Thanks," I said. "I did, too."

Owen looked up and grinned so hugely, I think Kerri actually took a step back. Clearly I had just made his decade.

"Cool. Okay. See ya," Owen said. Then he got out of there as fast as he possibly could.

"Wow," Kerri said. "I'm sorry. Was that a gentleman? I'm not sure I've ever seen one before."

"Yeah. He's kind of ridiculously sweet," I said, hugging myself.

"Well, we know one guy still wants you."

"And he's a totally safe bet."

"Unlike Mr. I-Have-a-Psycho-Ex over there," Kerri said.

Down the hall, Elena's voice was rising. Corey argued back. A couple of guys gave them a wide berth as Elena gesticulated wildly and Corey tried to calm her down. Is it wrong that my day was monumentally improved by seeing her upset?

"You know what? *Fine!*" Elena shouted finally, turning and storming off.

Corey rolled his eyes. He looked confused and embarrassed as he finally got to work on his locker combination.

"What was that all about?" I asked.

"I don't know," Kerri said. "But Corey's cute when he's flustered." She looked me up and down. "Huh. Now I get why you're so stressed. This is hard."

"Ya think?" I asked.

At that moment the school's PA system crackled to life, and Ms. Kruk, the school secretary, cleared her throat loudly over the microphone. "Attention, students. Thank you for participating in the homecoming court nomination process last Friday. The ballots have been counted, and the ten members of your homecoming court are now official."

An excited murmur traveled through the hallway as everyone paused to listen. I don't think I've ever heard my school so quiet.

"Your homecoming princes, from whom your king will be elected, are Logan Arnott, Corey Haskell—"

Corey beamed as a couple of guys slapped his hand.

"Joshua Marx—"

Kerri stuck a finger into her mouth and fake gagged.

"Kyle Stoller and Max Eastwood."

"Hey! Look at you, dating two members of the homecoming court!" Kerri said, slapping me on the back.

I rolled my eyes.

"Your homecoming princesses, from whom your queen will be elected," Ms. Kruk continued, "are Hailey Berkowitz, Grace Ricardo, Elena Marlowe, Sharon Stevens, and Kyla Danning."

"Shocker, shocker, shock, shock, shocker," Kerri said sarcastically.

I took a deep breath and sighed. Four Glossies and Elena, who was so gorgeous she even intimidated the Glossy clique. Not a single surprise on the whole list. Once again my school was as predictable as a Hollywood ending. It would be up to me to make homecoming even the slightest bit more interesting this year. Of course, with three prospective dates, it was already a hell of a lot more interesting than usual—at least for me.

"Excuse me! Step aside, freshmen! Senior class president coming through!"

I glanced over my shoulder at the cafeteria register to find Corey sidestepping the entire line with his tray full of food. He raised his eyebrows and grinned as he placed his tray down in front of mine.

"What do you think you're doing?" I asked as the lunch lady started ringing up his pasta and cookies.

"Presidential perks," he told me. "But I only cut in so I could talk to you."

I snorted but blushed. I had gotten so girly lately.

"So, there's this horror movie revival thing at the Hyperion this weekend," he said as he fished his wallet out of his backpack. "You wanna go? With me?"

Whoa. Talk about being blindsided. Corey was asking *me* out on a date? My knee-jerk reaction was to say yes. Yes! Of course I wanted a second date. But then I remembered Elena and her curl-tossing, head-tilting, hands-everywhere act, and my stomach turned.

"Listen, if you're worried about this whole thing messing up our friendship, I get it," Corey said. "Believe me. But I had a really good time on Saturday, and . . . I don't know. I think there's something—you know—*there*."

Okay, I wasn't even *thinking* about that. The screwing-up-the-friendship thing, I mean. At least I hadn't been at that specific moment, but now I was. What if we did go out and it didn't work and then we never spoke again? That would suck big-time. Meanwhile, Corey was giving me this cute, hopeful smile. It made me want to forget all logic, drop my Snapple, and kiss him right there.

I was getting mental whiplash trying to keep up with all my trains of thought. Seriously. And then there was still the little problem of . . .

"Um . . . what about Elena?" I asked.

Corey's brow creased. "What about her?"

The line was starting to stack up behind us and I could feel at least a dozen pairs of eyes boring into my neck, half-interested, half-annoyed. I slapped a couple of bucks down onto the counter for my Snapple and snacks and slid by Corey. He followed slowly and we paused by the wall.

"I . . . kind of . . . heard you guys talking this morning," I said, trying to load my words with meaning.

Corey scoffed. Twice. And glanced around as if someone might be watching him. "Oh, that. That was nothing." Very unconvincing. "So, do you want to go?"

I swallowed hard. I liked Corey. But what if Elena wasn't really out of the picture?

"It sounds cool," I said finally. "But I'm not sure what I have going on this week. Can I get back to you?"

Corey's face fell a little, but he recovered quickly. Ever the politician. "Sure. No problem. I'll see you after school."

It took me a second to figure that one out. "Oh! The homecoming meeting! Right!"

Corey gave me a quizzical look, then smiled and headed off for his table. I'm sure he thought it was a bad sign that his co-chair had spaced on our first meeting. Little did he know I had a zillion other things on my mind and he was one of them.

I navigated across the room and dropped down at my regular table with Kerri, Janice, and Lindsey. I was dying to talk to Kerri about Corey's invite, but I didn't want to get Janice and Lindsey started talking about the three-man-plan. Once they did, I knew it would be our only topic of conversation. And did I mention I don't like to be the center of attention?

"Hi, guys," I said quickly.

"Everything okay?" Kerri asked me, and I knew she had seen me and Corey talking.

"Yeah, fine," I mumbled.

"How's Corey?" Lindsey asked, raising her eyebrows as she flipped her blond hair over her shoulder.

"He's fine," I said, flushing.

"Did you figure out which one you're gonna pick yet?" Lindsey asked.

My red face got even redder.

"God, Lins. Look at her. She doesn't want to talk about it," Janice said, her green eyes wide behind her glasses.

"Sheesh," Lindsey said, rolling her eyes. "Just trying to make conversation."

But she dropped it and I shot Janice a grateful look. She tucked her short dark hair behind her ears and gave me a resolute nod. Maybe I was wrong about Janice and Lindsey wanting to gab about this nonstop.

Well, at least about Janice.

I sighed and pulled my sandwich out of my brown paper bag. I don't fully trust the cafeteria, and I cannot get by on bagels and salad like tons of girls in my class, so I usually bring the main course from home. I didn't realize how starving I was until I saw the nice wheat bread with the lettuce and tomato sticking out. Okay, it was time to relax and eat. I was about to take a big bite of my sandwich when suddenly the chair next to mine was pulled out and flipped around. Max Eastwood straddled it and faced me, resting his forearms on top of the chair. He had a couple of homemade CD cases in one hand, and he was grinning madly.

So much for food. Suddenly I was wondering if there was a closet around here somewhere.

"Hey, Quinn. I made you a present," he said.

I put my sandwich down and looked at my friends. Lindsey looked like she was about to burst from excitement. Janice was clearly irked at the interruption in our normal routine. Kerri was very obviously trying not to burst out laughing.

"Really?" I managed to say.

"CDs," he said, lifting them. "I downloaded all your favorite bands. And I put some other ones I thought you would like on there, too."

Shocked, I took the CDs and flipped through them—four in all—with cool graphic labels and at least twenty songs on each. I was—and I've never used this word before—flabbergasted.

"Wow, Max. Thanks," I said. "This must have taken you all weekend."

Max beamed. "It was worth it."

Kerri shot me an impressed look, and I stared back, my cheeks burning. She had told me everything was going to become clear, but as the day went on, my brain only got more and more muddled. So much for Kerri's idea of the guys taking themselves out of the running.

All I wanted to do after school was go home and crash in front of the TV. Honestly. It was as if the teachers had suddenly remembered that we were back in school, snapped out of their summer stupor, and slammed us with a ton of work all at the exact same time. Between imagining the piles of homework that awaited me and being completely preoccupied by the three-man-plan, I was exhausted. But I still had the homecoming meeting.

I didn't hear anyone coming up behind me, so when another hand fell on the auditorium door at the same time as mine, I nearly jumped out of my skin. Imagine the added inner freak-out when I realized it was Josh Marx.

"Hey," he said with a smile.

Oh, God.

"Hey," I replied.

He pulled the door open. "So, you had a busy weekend, huh?"

Why, oh, why was he suddenly noticing my existence?

His eyes sparkled as he shifted his books from one arm to the other. Was he *flirting* with me?

"What do you mean?" I asked, my pulse pounding.

He shrugged. "Just an observation."

Then he shoved a pen between his teeth with a smile and strode down the center aisle toward the stage. Trying to stop my mind from reeling, I followed, but I was only a few steps into the room when the sky pretty much fell.

Corey was there, obviously. But so was Max—sitting front and center. And Owen—huddled in a seat toward the back of the crowd. They were all there. All three of them. What were they doing here? The whole senior class was welcome, of course, but neither Max nor Owen had ever attended any Spirit Club or homecoming meetings before. Kerri and Lindsey turned around in their seats. Kerri shot me a look that fell somewhere between sympathy and mirth, while Lindsey just looked excited to see what would happen next, as if she was attending a play or something. Janice, of course, was absent. She didn't go in for stuff like school spirit.

What was I going to do? I glanced at the door behind me, but, considering I was co-chairing this meeting, escape didn't seem like a viable option. Somehow I made myself walk down the aisle. I could feel each of them watching me. I got to the stage, dropped my books up near the edge, and leaned back against it next to Corey, facing the seats.

Corey finished organizing some papers and winked at me. Max lifted a hand in a wave. Owen stared intently.

I was so totally nailed.

*Okay, okay, I can do this*, I thought, clinging to my notebook and pen as Corey started the meeting. *I just have to think about this logically. Pros and cons. Pros and cons.*

I doodled Corey's name on my notebook, followed by Max's and Owen's. Then I stared at them. Crap. I was becoming one of those girls I hated. Those girls who scribbled their crushes' names on every surface, drew hearts around them, and wrote their initials on the bathroom walls. Ew, ew, ew!

I took a deep breath and glanced out at the crowd. Max was right there. Four feet away. Smiling at me. Every inch of my skin sizzled. I think I might have even salivated. Okay. Pros about Max. There's the sizzling thing. And, damn, could he kiss. Every time I thought about him I wanted to be back in that closet. Plus he was really sweet and thoughtful, making me those CDs and everything.

But then . . . okay . . . cons. He was a little possessive of me at Stoller's party. And then he sat with me and my friends at lunch like we were already a couple. Kind of presumptuous on his part. . . .

"Quinn?"

My head snapped up as Corey waved a hand in front of my face. Everyone laughed. Kill me now.

"What? Sorry. I guess I spaced out for a second there," I said, hugging my notebook to my chest so he couldn't see my doodle.

"No problem," Corey replied. "Wanna go over the Spirit Show thing?"

"Oh, yeah." I flipped quickly though my notebook and came to the page outlining the Spirit Show points. Not that I needed them. I already knew what I wanted to say. But it gave me time to snap out of it. "Okay, as you all know, this year's theme is *Grease*. As seniors we get first pick of a song. Our skit, whatever it is, has to kick ass."

I earned a few hoots and hollers, particularly from Max. Blush.

"We cannot let the juniors beat us this year. Their 'In the Jungle' thing last year made us look like a bunch of amateurs. I don't know about you guys, but I think that the seniors should win this." Everyone cheered, and I started to feel a bit more comfortable. "I have a couple of ideas, but let's take suggestions first."

Corey nodded his approval and Josh instantly spoke up. "'Greased Lightning,'" he said confidently. "I'd *kill* as Kineckie."

"You are such a media whore," said Kerri, who has played minor parts in all the musicals that Josh and Elena have starred in. So she speaks from experience.

Josh made a face at her. Very mature.

"Okay, 'Greased Lightning' is on the board," Corey said. "What else?"

"'Summer Lovin',' " Elena Marlowe announced.

"Oh, and I guess you'd play Sandy," Kerri said.

"Well, it *was* my idea," Elena said.

Was it just me, or was she directing every comment and smile at Corey?

"Dude, 'Summer Lovin'' is *so* lame," Josh said, kicking back in his seat. "Everyone is gonna want to do it."

"Well, excuse me, spotlight hog, but your little song kind of leaves out the entire female population," Elena shot back.

"True," Kerri chimed in.

Okay, Elena was irritating, but she had a point.

"Elena's right," Corey piped in. "We should find something that will include whoever wants to participate."

I stared at Corey as he stepped up to Elena's defense and she gazed up at him with unmasked adoration. Apparently their earlier argument had already been forgiven and Corey was back on Elena's good side. I wasn't sure how much of this I could take. Corey was fun and hilarious and cool and gorgeous, but clearly Elena was making a move to get him back, and from the way he was looking at her and getting riled on her behalf, I wasn't too sure he didn't want *her* as well. I could really get slammed here.

Meanwhile, as the debate heated up, Owen simply sat back in his chair watching the proceedings with interest. Owen pros? What you see is what you get. No ex-girlfriends, no agenda, no ego. Just sweet, down-to-earth, shy Owen. With that killer smile. Cons? I just didn't feel that zing of attraction I felt around Max. Or even that exhilarating anticipation I felt around Corey. I felt *nada*, actually. But then, was that just because we hadn't kissed? I hadn't felt anything around Corey before our kiss, and now look at me. How could I rule Owen out without seeing if there was any chemistry?

Ugh! This was impossible!

"Uh . . . Quinn? Little help here?" Corey said.

I glanced up and saw that the meeting was in total chaos. Elena was shouting at Josh, who had his hands raised and an incredulous look on his face. Meanwhile everyone else was debating and laughing and groaning. Not good for the first ten minutes of our first meeting. I raised my fingers to my lips and whistled. It echoed off the walls, and everyone fell silent, staring at me. I cleared my throat.

"I do have one other idea," I said.

Elena crossed her arms over her chest and eyed me as

if I were the devil. Most everyone else looked interested. I launched right in.

"I was thinking we could do 'Beauty School Dropout,' but gender-bend it," I said. "Like . . . uh . . . Josh, you would be Frenchy in a pink wig and everything, and, Elena, you would be the guardian angel. And all the other angels could be guys dressed up in curlers and gowns, you know? I think it could be really funny."

There was a moment of silence, and then a few people laughed.

"That is hysterical," Kerri said loudly.

"What a great idea!" Lindsey chorused.

I so loved my friends.

"I love it!" Hailey Berkowitz interjected. "Omigod! We could get all the guys from the football and lacrosse teams and everything!"

"I could get the soccer team to come," Max piped in. "I think it is brilliant."

"No way!" Elena cried. "I wanted to be Sandy and wear the poodle skirt and everything. Now you're telling me—what? I have to wear an Elvis wig and bell bottoms?"

"Yes!" Corey said gleefully. "It's perfect! It's gonna bring down the house!"

I beamed. Take that, ex-girlfriend.

"Actually, it could be kind of funny," Josh conceded.

I beamed even more.

"You've gotta be kidding me," Elena said, crossing her arms over her chest. "There's no way I'm doing this. No way in hell."

"Good. Get out," Kerri said under her breath.

"Let's put it to a vote," Corey suggested. "All in favor of Quinn's idea?"

Every single person in the room raised their hand. Including Owen and Max and Corey. The only one who refused was Elena. I was so excited, I felt like jumping up and down. Not that I would ever do that.

"'Beauty School Dropout' it is!" Corey announced to thunderous applause.

"Corey!" Elena whined, widening her eyes at him. She might have even stamped her foot, but I couldn't really see from my angle.

"Sorry. Majority rules!" Corey said, raising his palms.

Elena glared at him, narrowed her eyes at me, then made a big show of gathering up her leather bag and perfectly distressed denim jacket. "Fine. If that's what you want to do, I quit. Good luck without your star."

Then she turned and stalked up the aisle, her high heels slowing her down just the tiniest bit.

"Too bad," I said, not meaning it at all. "Anyone want to volunteer to—"

"I will!" Kerri cried, jumping up. "I'll be the guardian angel."

I grinned. "Good. It's all yours."

"Perfect," Josh said, looking up at Kerri. "Guide me, my angel," he joked, smiling lasciviously.

Kerri rolled her eyes and dropped back into her seat.

"Okay, we'll start rehearsing at the next meeting," Corey said. "Good work, y'all. We'll see you on Thursday."

As soon as everyone started to get their stuff together, my heart slammed into my rib cage. This was it. The moment of truth in my three-man-plan. We were all in the same room together, and, from what I could tell, every last one of "my guys" was taking his dear, sweet time getting his butt out of his chair.

Oh, God. Oh, God, oh, God, oh, God. What was I going to do?

I turned around and fumbled with my backpack, slowly placing my notebook and pen inside. My hands trembled. My palms were covered with sweat. I was having trouble catching my breath, and I felt like I might throw up at any second. I was cornered. Triple-teamed. And there was no way out.

Okay. Deep breath. Come on. I could do this. With any luck at least one of them would leave the auditorium and wait outside. But when I finally turned around again, they were all there. Corey on my right near the piano, where his things were stacked. Owen emerging into the aisle. Max pushing his way out of his seat in the front row. Kerri stood at the back of the auditorium, gesturing frantically, offering in mime to pull the fire alarm. Part of me very much wanted to tell her to do it.

This was it. I had to do something, and I had to do it fast. But what? Who? Which guy should I choose?

# The Choice

*Okay,* I can't do this. It's just too difficult. So I'm leaving it up to you to choose. Here's a rundown to help you make an informed decision. Remember, you hold my romantic life in your hands.

. . . . . . . . . . . . . . . . . . . . . . . . . . . . . . . . . . . . . . . . . . . . .

## 1. Max

Pros: He's totally hot. And thoughtful. And athletic. And then there's that accent. Plus he makes me think about doing things that I've never thought about doing before, which is exciting.

Cons: He's a little over-the-top and kind of possessive. Plus he makes me think about doing things

that I've never thought about doing before,
which is scary.
Heartbreak risk level: *Moderate*

. . . . . . . . . . . . . . . . . . . . . . . . . . . . . . . . . . . . . .

# 2. Owen

Pros: He's mature, athletic, competitive, and also sweet.
He clearly loves his family. He's just as inexperienced in the sex area as I am—we think—so he
won't constantly be comparing me to other girls.

Cons: He's very shy and doesn't make my heart zing
the way the other guys do—at least not yet. Plus if
he's so inexperienced, who's gonna show me what
to do?

Heartbreak risk level: *Low*

. . . . . . . . . . . . . . . . . . . . . . . . . . . . . . . . . . . . . .

# 3. Corey

Pros: I already love him as a friend. I know everything
about him. He makes me laugh, he can board, and
I'm very comfortable around him. Also, his kiss
practically turned me to mush.

Cons: Elena, Elena, Elena. He may still want her, plus she's
freakin' hot. Who knows what the two of them have
done together? Could I ever measure up? Plus there's
the whole this-could-kill-the-friendship thing.

Heartbreak risk level: *Nuclear*

. . . . . . . . . . . . . . . . . . . . . . . . . . . . . . . . . . . . . .

$So$ there you have it. Who's it gonna be? Choose wisely. This is my heart you're messing with here!

If you choose $Max$,
keep reading.

If you choose $Owen$,
skip to page 135.

If you choose $Corey$,
skip to page 189.

# You Chose Max

# eight

I opened my mouth to ask Max to wait for me for a second while I talked to Corey—and I hoped Owen—but before I could even get out a syllable, Max grabbed me and twirled me around. What the—? I am not a girl who often gets twirled around.

"You killed! Everyone loved your idea!" Max cheered. His dark blue eyes gleamed with pride as he placed me down again. I started to fix my T-shirt, which had ridden up, and he pulled me in and kissed me, long and firm. "Nice work, baby."

Whoa. There went the knees again. God, he smelled good. *Maybe we should get out of here and . . .*

*Wait a second. I'm supposed to be doing something. . . .*

I heard the back door of the auditorium squeal as it

was shoved open, and I looked up just in time to see Owen's rapidly retreating varsity jacket. My heart thumped extra hard. Crap.

I glanced over my shoulder at Corey. He looked mighty confused. Not that I could blame him.

"Uh . . . Max?" I said, feeling ill. "I need to talk to Corey for a couple of minutes."

Max looked Corey over and stood up straight, the same way he had at the party with Josh. "Okay," he said finally. "Want a ride home?"

I grinned. "Sure."

"Good. I'll meet you outside." He took both my hands and gave me another kiss—this one on the cheek—before grabbing his bag and striding out. Sigh. He was even hot from behind.

*Reality to Quinn! Snap out of it! You have a friend to deal with here!*

I turned slowly and looked at Corey, biting my bottom lip.

"He called you *baby*," Corey said, half-surprised, half-amused.

I blinked. Somehow I hadn't processed that detail. "Yeah. I'll have to talk to him about that," I said with a laugh, trying to lighten the moment.

"So, I guess we're not going to the movies," Corey said.

He was taking this really well. No steam coming out the ears. No eye-contact avoidance. He just looked disappointed, which made me feel totally awful.

"I'm really sorry," I began. "We just kind of . . . I don't know . . ."

"Got together?" Corey supplied.

"Yeah."

*After choosing the two of you randomly from the senior class and taking you both for a test run. Plus Owen Meyer.* Ugh. Okay. I *was* awful. But at least it was over now.

"That's cool. Don't worry about it," Corey said, lifting his backpack onto his shoulder. "Hey, our date was just an experiment anyway, right?"

I flushed. It was more than that, really. But I had no idea how to explain that, so I kept my mouth shut. Corey smiled, and I couldn't have been more grateful that he was being so chill about this.

"Well, thanks," I said.

He shrugged. "No problem. So . . . better not keep Crocodile Dundee waiting."

"Yeah," I said.

For some reason I didn't move. Not that I wanted to drag this out, but what was I supposed to do once I got outside? Max was waiting for me. Max Eastwood. For me. Now that I had decided to be with him, what happened next? Nervous nausea for one thing.

"You okay?" Corey asked, his green eyes concerned.

"Oh, yeah. Fine," I said, attempting to swallow. Then I picked up my stuff and followed him out.

Max was sitting on the brick wall that ran along the stairs to the parking lot. He stood up as soon as I arrived and twirled his key ring around one finger. Corey took off for his own car, and Max and I were alone. Alone and together.

*Well*, I thought. *Here goes nothing.*

That night, after slogging through two hours of homework while trying not to daydream about Max, who had kissed me for a good five minutes in the car out front before my brother ran outside and knocked on the window, scaring the crap out of both of us, I decided to e-mail Owen. Cop-out city. I know. But since neither one of us was very good with talking, I thought it might be the best way to go. I took a big spoonful of Marsha Marsha Marshmallow ice cream and shoved it into my mouth before starting.

> Owen,
> I'm sorry about the Max thing. We're kind of dating now, I guess. I did have fun on our date, and I hope we can still be friends?
> WB
> Quinn

Wow. Poetic. I guess I'm not that great at writing either. Anyway, Owen must have been doing homework, too, because he e-mailed back right away. My breath caught in my throat when the little window popped up telling me I had a new message. I braced myself and clicked it open. Here's what *his* said:

> Quinn,
> It's fine. See you in school.
> Owen

He hated me, didn't he? But what did I expect? I tried to feel relieved, but I couldn't. This dating thing was hard. I was about to write back—I don't know what—when an instant message popped up from Max.

Aussie45: hey, baby! whatcha doin???

My grin nearly broke my face. I typed back.

Sk8_Quinn: homework . . . blah.
Aussie45: miss u already!!!

Really? Wow! But what was I supposed to write back to that? I guess:

Sk8_Quinn: miss u 2.

I felt so cheesy. But in a good way. This was what normal people did when they had boyfriends, right? Flirt on the computer?

Aussie45: listen 2 CDs yet???
Sk8_Quinn: listening right now.

Lie! I was listening to the new Aimee Mann downloads.

Aussie45: which song???

Oh crap! I grabbed my backpack and rummaged through

it, tossing out notebooks, pens, my gym T-shirt, until I found one of the disks. My hand was shaking as I read the playlist. Wait a minute. It wasn't like he could see me. Chill, girl. I took a deep breath and typed back calmly.

> Sk8_Quinn: modest mouse.
> Aussie45: sweet!!! so glad u like them!!!!

The boy really liked his punctuation marks.

> Aussie45: now i can imagine u sitting there looking beautiful listening 2 cds and thinking of me.

I cracked up laughing. How goofy was he? But romantic. I could be down with romantic. I was in a relationship here! Besides, he didn't need to know I was wearing chocolate-stained sweatpants and a baggy tank top, eating Ben and Jerry's right out of the carton.

> Sk8_Quinn: xactly!

And so began my first ever hour-long IM flirt session. I could get used to this having-a-boyfriend thing.

"So, is he going to be eating lunch with us *every* day now?" Janice asked, irritated. Janice was *always* irritated. We thought it had something to do with the fact that her father had moved to California last year and her mother had remarried this smarmy guy named Mitch who was always

94

staring at our chests when he talked to us. It was so gross that we all stopped hanging out at her house and she started hanging out at ours a lot more.

"Leave her alone," Lindsey said, ripping off a piece of her bagel. "She has a boyfriend."

"Aw, yeah!" Kerri said, laughing hugely.

Janice tucked her brown hair behind her ears and hunched over her lunch. "Fine. Whatever."

I glanced over my shoulder and saw Max loping toward us with that puppy-dog grin on his face. So cute. How could his presence irritate anyone?

"If it bothers you, Jan, we can move to the next table," I said under my breath.

"No, it's cool," she said with a sigh. Then she pulled out her iPod, stuck the headphones into her ears, and cranked it up.

Lindsey rolled her eyes and smiled. "Girl hates change."

"Ladies!" Max greeted us as he pulled out the chair next to mine and dropped into it. "My sweet," he said to me, taking my hand under the table and giving me a kiss.

"Wow! You guys already have pet names?" Lindsey asked.

"Just trying a few out to see what fits," Max replied.

"Well, she's anything but sweet," Kerri offered helpfully.

I responded by tossing a potato chip at her.

"I beg to differ," Max said, gazing at me as if the whole rest of the cafeteria had just melted away.

Holy heart palpitations. He ran his thumb back and forth across my palm. It was all I could do to keep from shivering. This was insane. This time last week no guy had ever held my hand before. No guy had ever really touched me, unless it was to tag me out in flag football or slam into me at the skate park. This was so freakin' cool.

"So, I was wondering . . . would you come see my game this afternoon?" he asked.

"Sure," I replied. I had nothing else to do. Except a pile of homework big enough to fill The Mill.

His face, if possible, lit up even more. "Cool." Then he leaned in, resting his chin on my shoulder, and whispered, "And maybe afterward we can go somewhere and be alone?"

I stopped breathing as whole parts of my body tingled with pleasure. I took a sip of water in an effort to cool myself down, but it didn't work. Somehow I refrained from dumping it over my head. Kerri was staring at me and trying not to laugh. I knew she knew what was going through my head. How was it possible that this person I had never spoken to before last week had this kind of effect on me?

"What do you think?" he asked, sending another shiver right through me.

"I'm totally there," I replied.

Soccer is huge in Garden Hills. Probably because our football team sucks to high heaven. The last time they had a winning season, I was still taking ballet lessons. Yeah. We're talking a *long* time ago. The soccer team, however, has been state champ three years running, and our guys are always landing scholarships to Big Ten schools. It was no wonder Max wanted to stay here.

I sat on the top bench of the metal bleachers as Max's game began that afternoon, surrounded by moms and dads and worshipping freshmen huddled in their little groups. When I saw Grace and Hailey, queens of the Glossies, making their way up the steps toward me, I didn't think anything of it—until they sat down right next to my battered backpack and skateboard.

"Hi, Quinn!" Hailey said.

"Oh . . . hi," I replied.

Hailey is one of those girls who will probably weigh eighty-five pounds for the rest of her life. She has tiny bones, skinny wrists, no ass at all, and a waist I could probably circle twice with my hip-hugging belt. Even her dark hair is fine and flat. Of course, she eats like a pig.

"Peanut-butter cup?" she asked, holding out an open bag of mini Reese's.

"Sure," I said. I took a couple, figuring that was going to be the extent of our conversation.

"So . . . you and Max Eastwood, huh?" Grace asked, leaning forward so that her ample cleavage almost grazed the head of the guy in front of her. "Go, you."

I looked at her for a second, expecting to see sarcasm and malice written all over her *Seventeen* cover-worthy face. I was shocked to find nothing there but awe. So, wait, the Glossies were actually talking to me and not mocking me?

"Thanks," I said, thoroughly confused and chagrined.

Now let me just explain here that I had no actual

evidence on which to base my theory that these girls were evil trolls who talked about people like me behind my back. I just always assumed that they were because, well, we were always talking about them behind their backs. I'm sorry! But it always seemed they had nothing on their minds other than makeup and clothes and the latest E! red carpet special. At least I'm woman enough to admit it.

A murmur ran through the crowd. I glanced at the field and was on my feet. Max had broken away from the pack and was racing down the field toward Franklin High's goal.

"Go! Go! Go!" Hailey shouted, jumping up and showering everyone in front of us with peanut-butter cups.

"Go, Max!" Grace shouted as well.

"Shoot it!" I screamed.

And he did. He slammed the ball, and it sailed into the far left corner of the net, right over the goalie's outstretched fingers. Everyone cheered, and Hailey hugged me as she bounced all around. I had to laugh. These girls were really into their soccer. Out on the grass, Max looked right at me and winked as he jogged back to midfield.

"Omigod! Did you see that?" Grace cried.

"He totally winked at you!" Hailey said enviously. "Oh! You are *so* lucky!"

I laughed as we all sat back down again and the spectators in front of us fished candy from their laps and hoods. A few people even unwrapped them and ate.

"Lost some of your snack there," I said to Hailey.

"No problem! I have another bag!" she said, opening her pink leather backpack to show me a stash of Snickers minis.

"Wow," I said.

"Let me know if there's anything you like, and I'll bring it next time," Hailey said.

"She will, you know," Grace told me. "Hailey is a total provider."

"Oh, okay," I said.

"I figure you'll be coming to lots of these things now," Hailey said, nudging me repeatedly with her elbow. This was too weird. All of a sudden me and the Glossies were best buddies. But I had to admit, they were kind of fun in their airheaded way. I was actually having a good time.

I smiled and watched as Max once again sprinted across the field with the ball, much to the pleasure of our fans. "Yeah," I said, feeling so giddy it bordered on obnoxious. "I guess I will."

The best part of the game was not finding out that Hailey Berkowitz and Grace Ricardo were actual humans. It wasn't even the fact that Max had scored both of Garden Hills' goals (the first one and the winning one) and had winked at me each time. Nope. It was the making out.

After showering and changing, Max met me outside the school. We drove over to the old, boarded-up roller rink, where we parked behind the huge neon roller skate that had long since been lowered to the ground. Everyone knew that this was the parking lot every basementless teenager in town came to when they wanted to fool around. I, of course, had never been there. By the time we arrived, the sun had started to go down, and the air sizzled with anticipation—and abject fear. What did he expect me to do here? What if I didn't know how to do it? What if he'd come here with the dozens of other girls he'd dated and he expected me to do the same things they had done? Panic city. When Max killed the engine, I was already out of breath.

"Is this okay?" he asked, his eyes already heavy.

One look at that totally Quinn-hungry expression and I forgot about all the other girls. Almost.

"Totally," I replied.

And then he grabbed me and kissed me.

Hi, my name is Quinn, and I'm a Max Eastwood junkie. Fifteen minutes into groping over the parking brake, Max broke away, got out of the car, and gestured at me to do the same. Somehow, through my hazy, muddled brain, I knew what he was thinking. My lips buzzing, I dove into the backseat with him so we could get even closer. Before I knew it I was on his lap with his hands tangled up in my hair. This was perfect. It was amazing. I could think about nothing other than the way his lips and hands and breath were making me feel. And it was *good.*

Then I shifted my weight, and something moved under my thigh. I turned ten shades of purple as I realized he was getting all excited. I had definitely never felt *that* before.

"What?" he asked, when I couldn't keep myself from giggling.

I swallowed and took a breath, mortified. "Nothing! Nothing!" I said, kissing him again quickly. "I just . . . I think I need to get home."

Not that I thought he was going to try to have sex with me. He hadn't even gone for my bra, thank God. (I was interested but still a little bit petrified at the same time.) I just wasn't sure I could deal with the constant reminder that he was raring to go.

"Oh, okay," he said. He looked a little crestfallen, but he smiled quickly and gave me one last peck before opening the side door. He held his jacket against his lap as he moved to the front, and he left it there the whole ride home. I kept my eyes trained out the passenger window and smiled privately. Maybe Owen wasn't the only gentleman out there.

I was heading for my locker after sixth period when Hailey and Grace slipped out of the bathroom, hair freshly teased, lips shimmering with newly slathered gloss.

"Quinn! Hey!" Hailey said, diving into her backpack as she caught up to me. She pulled out a tube of brownish lip gloss and handed it to me. "Here! I brought you something!"

I paused and looked around for Ashton Kutcher. "Lip gloss?"

"Yeah. Apparently I was experiencing a mind-freak when I bought it," Hailey said. "So not my color. But I think it'll look good on you!"

"She lives to give stuff away," Grace explained.

"Um . . . okay. Thanks," I said. I slipped the little tube

into my pocket and kept walking. Hailey and Grace fell into step with me. I caught a couple of mini-Glossies (sophomores who aspired to full Glossiness) looking at us in confusion. I didn't blame them.

"So, what are you wearing to the dance?" Grace asked.

"I don't know yet," I told them.

"You don't *know*?" Grace said with a gasp. "I've had my dress picked out since last spring!"

"Omigod! You have to let us take you shopping!" Hailey said, grabbing my arm with both her tiny hands. "It'll be so much fun."

I couldn't even imagine what a shopping spree with the Glossies would be like. Probably more grueling than the four-round county softball tournament. Luckily I was saved by the beep of my phone.

"Who's that?" Grace asked, excited.

"I don't know," I said, even though I did. My phone had been beeping and vibrating all day, and the messenger was always the same. It was getting kind of old, actually. Especially after I forgot to put it on vibrate during English class, and Mr. Williams confiscated it in front of everyone. I pulled the phone out and checked it.

Aussie45: u look hot 2day.

Oh, God. I tried to tuck it away, but Grace grabbed it right out of my hand. How embarrassing.

"Oh! He is *so* sweet!" she cried, facing the screen out so Hailey could see.

"Aw!" Hailey put in, taking the phone. "Here. I'll save it for you." She hit a few buttons, and her eyes widened. "Quinn! You have twenty messages from him in here!"

Busted. I grabbed the phone back and shoved it into my pocket. Okay, so maybe Max was being a little over-the-top, but he was just an emotional guy. It was fine. And it's not like it bothered me. Or it wouldn't if it stopped putting me into awkward situations.

"I gotta go," I said, catching a glimpse of Kerri waiting by my locker. She didn't look happy.

"Okay! See ya at the next game!" Grace called out.

"Call us about shopping!" Hailey added.

I trudged over to Kerri and blew out a hefty sigh as I dropped my heavy backpack onto the floor at my feet. Me, shopping with the Glossies. What was this world coming to?

"Wow! Look at Miss Popularity!" Kerri said.

I laughed. "I know, right? But they're pretty cool. We hung out at the soccer game yesterday."

"'Pretty cool'? Are you kidding me? Last week they didn't even know you existed," Kerri said.

"Hey, it's your fault they're talking to me at all," I said.

"How do you figure?" Kerri asked, eyebrows raised.

"If it wasn't for you, I wouldn't be dating Max, and I never would have gone to the soccer game, and I never would have been anywhere near the Glossies," I said matter-of-factly. "Take that, three-man-plan girl."

Kerri just looked at me, dumbfounded. "Touché."

Laura Drake, a girl from my homeroom, stopped at her

locker, next to mine. She popped it open, threw a few books inside, and started brushing her long brown hair, checking it in her locker mirror.

"Anyway, Max didn't know I existed last week either," I told Kerri. "And that seems to be working out."

I took out my cell and showed it to her.

"Holy crap! Has he had any time to eat or breathe?" she said, scrolling through the many messages.

"No clue," I said honestly.

"So, when do you think good old Aussie-forty-five is going to ask you to the dance?" Kerri asked, grinning.

"Max Eastwood?" Laura interjected, glancing around her locker door.

"Yeah," I said, taken off guard.

She scoffed and rolled her eyes. "Good luck."

Kerri and I exchanged a look. Where did *she* come from in this conversation?

"You're just bitter cuz he dumped you last year," Kerri said, handing my phone back.

"Yeah, right," Laura replied. "I dumped *him*. He got all . . . clingy," she said, adding a little shudder for effect. "I mean, he's nice and all, but he's, like, *always* there, *all* the time, breathing down your neck."

Something in my gut twisted uncomfortably. I looked down at the absurd list of messages on my phone.

"Plus he gets all insecure. Like, God forbid you should talk to another guy," Laura continued, flicking her hair behind her shoulders.

I remembered the way Max had reacted to me and Josh

talking at Stoller's party. And the suspicious way he had eyed Corey after the homecoming meeting. Was that what she meant?

No. Max was sweet. I liked how attentive he was. Really.

Laura fluffed her hair one last time, then slammed her locker door. "I'd get out early if I were you," she said, looking me up and down. "He only gets more golden retriever-like the longer it goes on."

"Right. Thanks," I said.

"Hey. We gotta look out for each other, right?" she said with a brief smile. Then she turned and flounced off, her Pantene-ad-worthy hair bouncing behind her.

"Ignore her," Kerri said. "All that mousse has seeped into her brain."

"Yeah," I replied, swallowing a lump in my throat. I held down the DELETE button on my phone and watched all the messages flash, then disappear. Then I shut it off. "Like you said, she's just bitter."


"Can I get you anything?" Max asked me the following night as we crowded into a booth at the diner with a bunch of other Spirit Show seniors including Kerri and Lindsey. We had just gotten out of a very successful rehearsal, and everyone was starving and giddy. We had already filled up four tables, and more people were on their way. "What do you want? Are you hungry?"

"Um . . . let me just think about it for a sec," I said.

"What's to think about?" Kerri said, sitting across from

me. "You always get the same thing here."

"Really? What is it?" Max demanded excitedly.

He bounced closer to me, looped his arm around my shoulders, and gave me a squeeze. My whole body tensed. I wasn't that used to PDAs to begin with. Hand-holding under the table was one thing, but right now he was practically sitting on my lap.

"I don't know. I might get something different," I said.

I pulled the menu toward me, which was tough considering how squished I was. I'm not sure why I was being so difficult. Kerri was right—I always got a burger or chicken fingers. But Max had been on top of me all day, asking me all kinds of personal questions, and after four text messages during first period alone I had been forced to turn my phone off and leave it in my locker all day. I wanted him to back off a little.

"I just want to know everything about you. Is that so wrong?" Max asked.

Lindsey looked at me all dopey-eyed. "Oh! That is *so* cute!"

That seemed to be the opinion of the general female population. And maybe it *was* cute. Maybe I just had to relax.

"Okay. I'll get chicken fingers and fries," I said.

"Great. One chicken fingers and fries," Max said in a satisfied way. He plucked the menu out of my hands and scanned the pages as he scooted away a few inches. "Now, what am I going to have?"

See? He's totally normal.

The air-conditioning vent over my head whirred to life and blasted me with a *whoosh* of cold air. I shivered and crossed my arms over my chest.

"Are you cold?" Max asked. "Do you want my jacket?"

"No, I'm fine," I told him.

"I could ask them to switch it off," he suggested, looking around for a waiter. "They don't have to keep it arctic in here. Doesn't anybody work in this place?"

I widened my eyes at Kerri.

Kerri looked back at me and mouthed, *What?*

Maybe I was overreacting. I had to put Laura Drake and her stupid opinions out of my head.

"Don't worry about it," I said to Max. "If I want them to turn down the air-conditioning, I'll ask them."

Not that I would. Cool air could never bother me enough to make me create a scene. And I didn't want Max creating one either.

"Just trying to take care of you," Max said, kissing me on the cheek.

"Aw!" Lindsey intoned.

*Dial it down, girl! Don't encourage him!* I thought much to my dismay.

"So, what do you want to drink?" Max asked me.

Luckily his phone stopped me from answering that question. It let out a shrill ring and as soon as he checked the caller ID, he slid out of the booth. "Be right back," he said, kissing me once again. The moment he was gone, my whole body relaxed.

"What's up?" Kerri asked.

"Nothing," I said with a sigh. I really didn't feel like talking about it.

"Quinn, is this about what Laura—"

"Quinn Donohue!" Josh Marx sang my name as he dropped into the seat Max had just vacated. He reached out and gave me a quick but firm squeeze. Yes, a squeeze. "Can I just tell you how much this 'Beauty School Dropout' thing is going to rock? You are a genius!"

"Thanks," I said.

Unshockingly, I was the same color as the ketchup bottle. But I am proud to say that my insides weren't doing the same spastic gymnastic routine they would have a few weeks ago. Huh. Apparently all my hormones had decided to focus on Max.

Max. I thought of our day in the roller-rink lot and smiled happily. Okay, who cared if he was a little out-there with his affections? If he could make me feel like that *and* make me stop liking Josh Marx after five years of unrequited love, how bad could he be?

"We are gonna kick the juniors' ass!" Josh cheered, earning a round of raucous catcalls. "Asses. Ass. Whatever! We're gonna kick it!"

Everyone laughed, and Josh settled in, resting his arm on the back of my seat. Kerri eyed me in an amused way, and I realized I was sitting forward rigidly, avoiding all contact with him. I guess he still made me a *little* nervous. I didn't even notice Max had come back inside until his shadow fell over the table.

"Hey, man," he said to Josh. "You're in my seat." Max

109

didn't sound like his normal boisterous self.

"Sorry, dude," Josh said, raising his hands. He slid out of the booth and stood up, coming chest-to-chest with Max, who didn't move an inch out of the way. They stared at each other for a moment before Josh finally cracked a smile and loped back to his table.

"Quinn? May I talk with you for a second?" Max asked.

Uh-oh. Total hollow-stomach moment. I glanced at Kerri, who looked like she was trying not to laugh, and followed Max over to the counter by the wall.

"What was that about?" Max asked the moment we were alone.

"What was *what* about?" I asked.

"Why is it every time I turn around, you're talking to Josh Marx?" he asked.

Can you say *ironic*? "Believe me, I hardly ever talk to Josh Marx," I assured him.

"Look, if you want to see other people, just tell me," Max said. His eyes were serious, and his expression was all tight. "Don't lead me on."

I balked. I had no idea what to say. I wouldn't know how to lead someone on if I wanted to. "I'm definitely not leading you on," I told him.

Relief flooded his face and he took my hand, lacing his fingers through mine. "Good. It's just . . . I really like you, you know? So much."

Okay, he really was sweet. "I like you, too," I said.

He gazed into my eyes, and I waited for him to say something else, but he didn't. He just kept staring. And staring. And staring. In this totally love-struck way. Finally I had to look away myself before he really started to weird me out. For a girl who had hardly ever been noticed before, that kind of adoration was a little disturbing.

"Oh! There's the waitress!" I said, pointing at our table, relieved for the diversion. "We should go order."

I took one step, but he held on to my hand and pulled me back. Then he kissed me so deeply and energetically that I forgot all about the diner and the twenty kids from my class acting as spectators. I even forgot about the extreme mushiness and drama.

Max's kisses could pretty much make me forget about anything.

Max had another home game after school on Friday. I decided to skip it this time, even though it was totally obvious he expected me to go. He spent the entire morning sending dozens of text messages about how I was his good luck charm and he was going to score three goals for me this time instead of just two. By third period I turned off my phone again, and then I spent my lunch hour in the library pretending to study. I needed some time alone to think. Was Max actually freaking me out, or was I only noticing it because Laura had said something?

After school I sent him a quick text message telling him I couldn't make it, then went straight to the skate park. That's where I always do my best thinking.

After about an hour of speeding back and forth on my board, practicing kickups and 360s and watching other skaters, I was feeling a lot better. This was no big deal, right? So Max was a little overzealous. He was from another country. Maybe they did things differently over there. And what was I complaining about anyway? That one of the hottest guys in school liked me enough that he wanted to be with me all the time? I could only imagine what the boyfriend-free population would say: *"Cry me a river, honey."*

I shook my head and smiled as I paused at the top of the big ramp and tipped back down again, the sun on my face and my own velocity whipping my ponytail back. I was just being silly. Max was my first boyfriend. I was going to get used to this.

Atop the incline this guy I knew only as "Baker" jumped onto his board and started down. He was a little close to me so I began to veer out of his way at the bottom of the bowl. Just as I made my move, I looked up and saw Max standing by the fence, still in his grass-stained soccer uniform. What the heck was he doing here?

"Hey! Watch out!" Baker shouted.

Max's eyes widened, and I whipped around just in time to see Baker's padded elbow coming right at my face. The next thing I knew, I was flat on my back with the wind knocked out of me. My head throbbed under my helmet, and Baker's foot was lodged under my shoulder. It all happened so fast, I wasn't sure if it was his fault or mine.

*Probably mine,* I thought. The second Max's face appeared above mine, blocking out the sun, I revised: *Definitely mine.*

"Are you all right?" Max asked.

*Okay, breathe,* I directed myself. I struggled to pull in air, and my lungs burned until I coughed. As I pushed myself onto my elbows, I wheezed.

"Oh, my God. Quinn! Can you breathe!? Should I call an ambulance?" Max asked.

I shook my head no, still coughing, and was eventually able to choke out a couple of words. "No ambulance. Fine."

Baker picked himself up and dusted himself off. "You okay?" he asked.

I nodded. "Sorry." I stood up and unbuckled my helmet. My jeans were ripped just below the knee and I had a scrape, but that was the only damage.

"Are you hurt? Did you break anything?" Max asked, checking me over.

"I'm fine. Really," I said.

"You gotta watch where you're going, Quinn," Baker said.

"I know," I said, nodding. "My bad."

"It wasn't your fault," Max said. "This guy came outta nowhere."

"Yo, dude. Back off," Baker said.

"Really, Max, it was me. I was . . . distracted," I told him. *By you,* I added silently.

Max shot Baker a venomous look, and I realized things could get ugly here. I grabbed Max's arm and pulled him away, limping a little. The last thing I wanted was Max to go off fighting for my honor or something.

"You *are* hurt!" Max cried as I led him to a picnic table.

"Come on. We're going to the hospital."

I laughed. I couldn't help it. This injury was nothing a little Bactine and a Band-Aid couldn't handle. "I'm fine. *Really*. Calm down," I told him, sitting on the bench.

Max pushed his hands into his sweaty hair and hovered over me. "I'm sorry. It's just . . . when I saw that guy coming toward you, my life flashed before my eyes."

"Really?" I said with a laugh.

Max's eyes darkened. He was totally and completely serious. This was getting freakier by the second.

"Max, I'm okay. This kind of stuff happens all the time," I said.

"Well, then, maybe you should take up a different hobby," he said.

I took a deep breath. He had to be kidding. "What are you even doing here?" I asked.

He crouched in front of me and checked under the ripped flap of my jeans, inspecting the scrape. "I was worried when you didn't show up for my game," he said, looking up at me through his long bangs. "I couldn't concentrate. I didn't know where you were."

I studied his face, trying to figure out where all this was coming from. I'd barely known him a week, and he wanted to know where I was every second? He gazed back at me, his expression almost impossibly earnest.

"I sent you a text message. Didn't you get it?" I asked.

His brow creased. "No. I guess not."

"Well, I did and I'm here," I said, at a loss for anything else to tell him.

114

Max smiled slightly and pushed himself up to kiss my lips. For the first time I didn't go all weak and fluttery. "Come on," he said, standing and offering his arm. "I'll take you home so you can get cleaned up."

I glanced past him at the few skaters still on the ramps and felt a powerful need to get back out there and clear my mind again. But he was right. I couldn't skate until I took care of my wound. With a sigh I ignored his outstretched hand and stood up.

I had a feeling I was going to need some serious alone-time to figure out where this Max thing was going and if it was anywhere I wanted to be.

# ten

I managed to snag the "me time" I needed and made it through the rest of the weekend without seeing Max, but it wasn't easy. When we got to my house on Friday evening, he came inside for a snack. I told him I had a big family get-together on Saturday and that my dad, my brother, and I always spent Sunday together. (One big lie, one half truth. Jack has no interest in football unless it's Arena, where the players are pretty much allowed to kill and maim.) Max got so excited at this news, I'm ninety-nine percent sure he expected to be invited to one or both events. So I distracted him by pretending to choke on an Oreo and that did the trick.

Still, by the end of the night on Sunday I had no fewer than forty-five—yes, *forty-five*—e-mails from him and another half dozen voicemail messages. On Monday morning, for the first time in my life, I was dreading going to school for a reason that had nothing to do with being unprepared for a test.

When I saw the little crowd gathered around my locker, I knew I was in for it. Grace spotted me over one shoulder and nudged Hailey, and they both moved out of the way, grinning Cheshire-cat style. I paused when I saw what had attracted all the attention. Taped to my locker were two huge heart-shaped balloons and a red rose with a pink card. My body temperature skyrocketed, and I ducked my head as I ripped the card down. A few of the skate park guys smirked as they walked past.

Turning my back to them, I opened the card and read:

Sweet Quinn,
Will you do me the honor of attending the
homecoming dance as my date?
Love,
Max

"What's it say!? What's it say!?" Hailey demanded, bouncing up and down in her stiletto-heeled shoes.

Grace snatched the card out of my hand and scanned it. "Now we *have* to go dress shopping."

"I . . ."

My entire throat was dry. Everyone was staring at me. This was my worst nightmare.

"All right, people! Move it along! Nothing to see here!"

Kerri Lawrence to the rescue! She clapped her hands as she shoved through the crowd. "Let's go! Let's go! Let's go! Bell's about to ring! Get a move on!"

A few people groaned and rolled their eyes, but they started to disperse. Soon I was able to breathe again, though I still felt like tearing out of there and not looking back.

"Kerri!" I whimpered, gesturing at the huge balloons. "What am I going to do?"

"Quinn! Come on! It's romantic," she said, taking the rose down and twirling it. "You gotta love a guy who makes the big gesture."

"No, *you* gotta love a guy who makes the big gesture," I said under my breath. "I'm more of a little gesture person. Or no gesture at all. Gesture-free is fine by me."

"You're rambling," Kerri said flatly. "If you wanted someone subdued, you shoulda gone with Owen."

"You're right. Owen would never do something like this," I said. "Maybe I should've picked him."

"If you'd picked him, you'd be sleeping off your boredom somewhere right about now."

I stared up at my distorted reflection in the silver side of the balloons. She had no idea how attractive that idea sounded.

At that moment Max came around the corner, looking all sheepish and hopeful. He was wearing a blue shirt that made the color of his eyes visible from yards away, and he looked gorgeous. Too bad I wanted to wring his neck.

"Hey, baby," he said, planting a kiss on my lips. "I

118

missed you this weekend."

All I could say was "Yeah."

Kerri backed up to the wall behind him and waited. He took both my hands and looked deeply into my eyes. This was getting old fast. From the corner of my eye I saw Laura Drake smirk as she approached her locker, batting the balloons out of the way to get to it.

"So, what do you say?" Max asked me. "Will you go with me?"

A few people were still milling around. Kerri shrugged as if to say, "What better offers do you have?"

I sighed, knowing Laura was taking it all in and expecting me to cave. But what was I supposed to do, turn him down in front of all these people? In front of his ex-girlfriend?

"Uh . . . sure," I said. "Sounds great."

Max grinned and enveloped me in a tight hug. My feet even left the floor. Then he kissed me right there in the hall, and all the spectators applauded.

"Hope you're stocked up on kibble," Laura said under her breath.

Kill me. Seriously. Kill me now.

"You're going dress shopping with Hailey and Grace!?" Kerri demanded after lunch.

"I'm sorry! They won't leave me alone about it!" I cried as we climbed the steps out of the cafeteria. "You should come. Please? You can't leave me alone with them. They'll put me in some Barbie-doll dress, and I won't be able to talk my way out of it."

Kerri stopped walking and leaned back against the hallway wall. She crossed her arms over her chest and kicked at the floor with the toe of her shoe. "I don't know. Wouldn't want to trip you on your climb up the social ladder."

I had to laugh. "Kerri. If there's one thing I care less about, it's social ladders. I want you to come. Please?"

Kerri just sighed and looked off down the hall. I couldn't believe how much this whole Hailey and Grace thing was bothering her.

"I have to go with them. You know I'm incapable of saying no," I told her. "Witness the fact that I'm going to the homecoming dance with a guy who may or may not be a psychotic stalker."

Finally she looked me in the eye. "All right," she said. "I'll go."

"Thank you!"

"But for the record, I don't think Max is a psychotic stalker," she said. "I just think he's kind of clueless. And he's still ridiculously hot."

"You got me there," I said with a sigh. Unfortunately I was starting to think that "ridiculously hot" could only get a girl so far.


Apparently seeing Quinn Donohue in taffeta is a coveted entertainment ticket, because when my mom heard about the shopping spree, she insisted on coming along as well. Kerri had already picked out a halter dress in her signature red for her date with Mike Bonner, so everyone in my little group was truly shopping just for me. When the five of us walked into Macy's, it felt like I had an entourage, everyone trailing behind me, pointing things out for my inspection. But from their choices, it didn't seem as if any of them actually had *me* in mind.

"Oh! Quinn! What about this?" my mother said, picking up a pink strapless dress with a huge poofy skirt.

"Okay, this isn't the Oscars and I am not Hilary Duff," I said.

She put it back on the rack and kept browsing. I know my mom loves me, but sometimes I think she really wanted a girly-girl.

"You have to try this on!" Hailey cried, running over with a black thing that was about the size of a bandanna.

"Hailey, I don't think that would cover her ass," Kerri said.

"Thanks a lot," I replied. But it was true. It might have made a cool belt if she rolled it up.

"Check *this* out," Grace said, producing something in blue leather with laces on the bodice.

"Um . . . no," my mother said, appearing out of nowhere.

My phone beeped, and I ignored it. I knew it was Max with another embarrassing lovey-dovey message. It beeped again and everyone stared at my pocket.

"You gonna get that?" Kerri asked.

"No. I think I'm going to go look over here," I said, pointing at a wall full of basic black dresses.

121

"Please try on something in a color," my mother begged.

I sighed as my phone beeped *again*. "How about you pick out three dresses and I'll promise to try them on?" I said. "Just three."

"Yes!" my mom cheered. Then she attacked the racks like a poacher on the prowl.

Hailey, Grace, and Kerri followed me over to the wall of black, and we started inspecting the dresses. My phone beeped yet again. Was it just me, or did it sound more and more sickening each time?

"Uh, Quinn? Why aren't you answering that?" Grace asked.

"What if it's Max?" Hailey put in.

"That *why* she's not answering it," Kerri told them.

"What?" they both blurted out.

"Thanks for that," I told Kerri.

She shrugged by way of apology. Suddenly Grace and Hailey were on me like vultures on roadkill.

"Are you mad at him?"

"What's going on?"

"Are you two breaking up?"

I extricated my arms from their grips and tried to lower my tense shoulders.

"No, we're not breaking up," I assured them. From the level of their relief you'd think I'd just told them they were both going to stay thin and cellulite-free for all eternity. "It's just . . . a lot," I explained. "He calls me every ten minutes and texts me every two. I need a break."

Grace and Hailey exchanged a confused look. "A

break? From Max Eastwood?" Hailey said. "He's, like, the hottest guy in school."

"Yeah, Quinn. Who died and made you Angelina Jolie?" Grace put in, flipping some hangers vehemently.

I wasn't even sure what that meant, so I just let it go. A frigid iciness descended on the dress department, and I shot Kerri a "help me" look. She rolled her eyes and pulled out a hideous purple number that looked like it had been made out of a hundred rags sewn together with sequined buttons.

"Omigod! You totally have to try this on!" she trilled in a perfect Grace imitation.

Taking her cue, I widened my eyes and grabbed the dress. "This is *so* me!" I cried.

Grace actually sneered. "You guys need professional help, like, stat." She took Hailey's wrist. "We'll be over by the jeans."

She tugged Hailey away, and they scurried off as fast as they could in their stiletto-heeled boots. The moment they were gone, Kerri and I cracked up laughing.

"What was that?" I said, grasping a round rack for support. "I tell them I don't feel like talking to Max, and it's like they just found out I'm plotting to burn down *Vogue*."

"Hey, you're the one who wanted to hang out with them," Kerri said.

"No way! They wanted to hang out with me!" I replied.

"Well, I think we've solved that problem," Kerri said, laughing.

Clearly she was feeling a lot more relaxed now that the

Glossies were gone. In fact, so was I. I had to remember to keep to my own kind. At least on important matters like—shudder!—dress shopping and—shudder! heave!—guy-talk. Weird. When did I become an actual girl?

Just then my mom reappeared with three dresses folded over her arm. From where I was standing, they didn't even look that bad. She gestured at the dressing room behind me with a grin. "Shall we?"

"We shall," I replied.

"Quinn, you look so hot," Kerri said for the fourteenth time as we sat on the couch in my family room with Mike, waiting for Max to arrive.

"She does, doesn't she?" my father said.

"Ew, Dad!" I cried.

"I was just agreeing!" he said. He snapped a picture, then walked around to the side of the couch and snapped another one. All of a sudden he was like Mr. Paparazzi. "You're gorgeous."

"Yeah, definitely," Mike said, nodding as he eyed me up and down.

"Hey! Drool this way, buddy," Kerri said, snapping her fingers.

Mike reddened and flashed her a "snagged" smile. Kerri *was* looking very drool-worthy in her tasteful-yet-sexy red dress. Plus she had spent all day having extensions put in so her hair hung straight and lush down her back like Beyoncé's.

"Just complimenting your friend," Mike said sheepishly, giving her a peck on the cheek.

"Well, thanks," I said, smoothing the skirt of my dark blue dress. "I appreciate the effort."

I had gone with one of the dresses my mom picked out. It had simple spaghetti straps and an A-line skirt (that's what Mom had called it) and came just below my knees, so I didn't have to worry too much about sitting improperly by mistake. My hair was up in a chignon, thanks to Mom, and Kerri had come over early to do my makeup again. With low black heels and a black purse I had borrowed from Lindsey, I was ready to go.

Except that I was nervous as hell. The Spirit Show had gone off without a hitch yesterday afternoon, and the entire audience had freaked for Josh and Kerri's performances. But what if we didn't win? (The results of the voting were being announced tonight.) Or what if something horrible happened at the dance? Corey and I and the rest of the committee had worked so hard. I couldn't take it if anything went wrong.

And then there was Max. Such a wild card. I half expected him to show up in a stretch limo ready to whisk me off to Vegas for some 'til-death-do-us-part scenario. You never knew with this guy.

The doorbell rang, and I jumped out of my seat. My skin tingled with excitement and, like, a *smidge* of dread. I heard my mom welcoming Max into the front hall, and then there he was in the doorway.

*Holy supermodel, Batman.* Okay, everyone was right. Max Eastwood was the picture-perfect date. He wore a dark blue suit that looked like it had been made for him and a light blue tie over a pristine white shirt. His smile was like something out of a toothpaste commercial.

"Hi, everyone," he said, lifting a hand. "Quinn . . . wow."

I flushed pleasantly. Okay. Maybe I could handle ten million messages a day and constant PDAs. *Look* at this guy!

"Get together for a picture!" my dad ordered as my mother stepped up next to him. She looked like she was about to cry as Max put an arm around me and we posed.

Kerri flashed me two thumbs-up as she and Mike joined us in front of the fireplace for a few more shots, pressing me closer to Max. God, he smelled good.

"You're gorgeous," he whispered into my ear, his breath sending a shiver right through my body. Suddenly I was re-experiencing that primal urge to jump him.

Not in front of the parents, of course.

He slipped his hand into mine and squeezed. My heart pounded extra hard.

*Okay*, I thought. *Maybe I can make this work. . . .*

. . . Or maybe not.

"All I want to do is touch your skin," Max said, sliding his fingers across my cheek and down my neck as we stepped back and forth in the center of the dance floor. "This hair . . . this, this *ear*."

"My *ear*?" I blurted.

"It's perfect. You have an absolutely perfect ear."

Oh, geez. I was gonna hurl. It had been like this from

126

the second we arrived. He loved my eyes, my lips, my fingers, my ankles. Next he was going to be complimenting my armpits. Luckily the song ended, and a fast one started up. I removed myself from his arms and trudged off the dance floor. Max, of course, followed on my heels.

"You should wear dresses more often," he said, reaching for my hand. "You look so beautiful in dresses."

"I don't like them," I said flatly, heading for the punch bowl.

"Oh, but you look so—"

"Beautiful, I know," I said.

I grabbed a paper cup full of punch and sucked half of it down. Max leaned against the gym wall and gazed at me in a way that made me think he'd just been sprung from a cult compound in Utah.

"What?" I said.

"Do you think we'll be together forever?" he asked.

*I don't think we're going to be together through the next song,* I thought.

"You should apply to UCLA with me," he said.

"What?" Being with Max meant asking one-word questions quite often.

"Apply there. And to UMass and Miami and—"

"Why?" There was another one.

He reached for my hand, and I tried to pull it away, but he caught me and pulled me toward him.

"So we can be together," he said, running his fingers down my cheek again.

This was starting to make me cringe.

127

"What if I don't want to go to UCLA or UMass or—"

His bottom lip jutted out. "You don't want to be with me?"

I sighed. "Max—"

Suddenly I felt a presence at my side and looked up. It was Owen. I can't express the depth of the relief I felt at the sight of him. I hadn't spoken to him since I blew him off via e-mail, but something about him was comforting. Maybe because I knew for sure he was sane, while my date was freaking me out more and more by the second. Owen looked great in his black suit, even if it was a size too small. His blue shirt peeked out a bit too much around the wrists, and his red tie was a tad short. But he was a sight for sore eyes.

"Hi, Owen!" I said happily. I tore my hand away from Max's.

"He-hey Quinn," he said, growing a little bit blotchy.

Max stood up straight and squared his shoulders the way he always did when other guys were around.

"I . . . uh . . . ." Owen's eyes darted to Max. "I was wondering if you wanted to dance. Once. With me."

"Definitely!" I replied, placing my punch cup down.

Owen's grin could have melted the ice sculpture.

"Quinn," Max said. "May I speak to you for a moment?"

"Actually, Max, can it wait?" I said.

His face went all hangdog. "I thought *I* was your date."

Oh, he had to be *kidding* me!

"Owen, could you just hang on for one second?" I asked.

"Sure." He walked a few paces away and put his hands in his pockets, surveying the dance floor.

I sighed and turned to Max. "What's up?"

"I thought you came here to dance with me," he said. "Don't you *want* to dance with me?"

He looked at me with his puppy-dog eyes and reached for my hands again. This time I shoved them both under my arms.

"No, actually, I don't."

Whoa. Did I just say that?

"What?" Max asked, shocked.

Now that I had started, there was no turning back.

"Max, look, I'm sorry. I don't think this is working out," I said. My heart was slamming around in my chest and sweat broke out along my hairline, but I held my ground.

"What? How can you say that?" he demanded. "Quinn! I love you!"

My jaw dropped. It was all I could do to keep from laughing. This guy was insane! He didn't even *know* me. Especially not if he thought I would give up boarding or start wearing dresses or invite him to family gatherings when I'd only known him a couple of weeks.

"No," I said. "You really don't."

"But I do!" he protested. "You're all I think about! You can't break up with me, Quinn! I don't know what I'll do without you!"

He sounded so insane, but in that moment I really think he believed what he was saying. Which made it even more insane.

"Max, you're an amazing guy," I told him, racking my brain for the right thing to say. "It's . . . it's not you. It's me!" I can't believe I just said that. "I . . . can't be in a serious relationship right now. I need . . . I need space. If you really love me, you'll . . . you'll give me what I need."

I had no idea what I was talking about, but I had the distinct feeling that I owed it all to watching hours of mind-numbing WB marathons with Kerri.

Even though I was spouting total blather, it seemed to hit a chord in Max. He took a deep breath and looked at me longingly. "If you love something, set it free. If it comes back to you, it is yours. If it does not, it never was."

*What?* I stared at him for a second. "Does that mean I can go?"

Max nodded resolutely. "Good-bye, Quinn."

"Bye, Max," I said, somehow keeping a straight face. Then I walked back over to Owen and led him to the dance floor.

"What was that all about?" Owen asked as a nice, new slow song welcomed us into the throng.

"I just had my first breakup!" I said.

Owen's brow creased. "You seem very excited about that."

"I am!" I said with a smile.

Owen shrugged and put his arms around my waist. Kerri bounded over from the makeshift stage where she had been hovering all night, watching as the school cast their votes for Spirit Show and homecoming king and queen.

130

"What happened?" she demanded. "Max just slammed out the side door on the verge of tears!"

I'd made him cry? Oh, man.

"Is he okay?" I asked.

"Well, Grace Ricardo chased after him, so I think he will be," Kerri said, rolling her eyes.

I laughed. "Well, good. She can have him."

"Grace and Max? Now, that makes sense," Owen said matter-of-factly.

And just like that he put the last two weeks into perspective. Max and I never made sense. No matter how hot he was or how amazing it felt when we fooled around, we were never going to mesh in the real world. But thanks to him I now knew what it was like to be seriously kissed, I could say that I once had a boyfriend, and I knew what to avoid next time I went looking for love. Plus I was on the dance floor with my best friend and a cute, sweet, *normal* guy.

All in all, I think I came out of this one on top.

## The End

(or not . . . turn the page!)

# The Choice Redux

**Do** *you* agree with my little assessment? Did I come out on top here, or could I have done better? If you want to try again with a new guy, go back to page 85. And choose right this time! Sheesh. Do I have to do everything around here?

*You Chose Owen*

# eight

I was trapped. Corey eyed me expectantly. Max had this excited puppy-dog look plastered on his face. Owen pushed a hand into the pocket of his jeans and raised his eyebrows at me. I had no idea what to do. What to say. Whom to talk to first. So I did the only logical thing that came to mind.

I made a break for it.

Just as Max reached in to hug me, I tore up the aisle and grabbed Owen's arm. My heart was pounding like I was some in-season animal under hunter fire.

"Wanna get out of here?" I asked.

But I didn't give him time to answer. He tripped backward as I hauled him up the aisle.

"Everything okay?" Owen asked as I released him and we stepped into the sunlight.

"Sure. Fine. Why?" I asked, glancing over my shoulder.

"Uh . . . no reason," Owen said, eyeing me as if he was afraid I might suddenly explode.

"I'm hungry. Are you hungry?" I asked. I was, in fact, starving, but mostly I wanted to get the heck out of there before either Max or Corey could catch up to us.

"I can always eat," Owen said.

"Good. Let's go get some pizza," I suggested.

"Cool," he said with a nod. "My car's over there."

Mode of escape! I practically jogged to Owen's Subaru and didn't feel safe again until I was hunkered down inside.

Owen got in and started the engine. "So . . . where do you want to go? Tino's?"

"Sounds good," I replied.

Owen smiled, and a little rush of excitement shot through me. This was the guy I'd chosen for better or for worse. I couldn't wait to see what happened next.

"Your skit idea is great, by the way. It's gonna be hysterical," Owen said as he lifted his slice of pizza.

"Ya think?" I asked, pleased.

"Are you kidding? Josh Marx in drag? The guys will go nuts and the girls will probably love him even more for having the guts to do it," Owen said. "He'll be pied-pipering the girls of the freshmen class around for the rest of the year."

I blinked. "Wow. You sure know our audience."

"Just because I don't talk much doesn't mean I don't listen," Owen said with a small smile. "People say all kinds of things when they forget you're there."

That comment made me both sad and intrigued. Sad because of how lonely it must make him feel. Intrigued because, hell, if it was true, what kind of stuff had he *heard*? Who knew Owen Meyer had so many levels?

"So, one of the things you've learned is that every girl in school has a crush on Josh Marx?" I said, trying not to blush and give myself away.

"It's been going on since the third grade," Owen said. He looked off above my head, feigning wistfulness. "The mojo was always strong with that one."

I nearly spit out my soda. I couldn't believe this was Owen Meyer talking.

"He did always get more valentines than the rest of us," I recalled.

"And didn't he, like, date a seventh-grader back in fifth?" Owen widened his eyes. "Scandal."

I laughed and took a bite of my pizza. The fact that Owen had a semi-caustic sense of humor was a fabulous revelation. I really liked this kid. I think even Kerri would like this kid. If he could ever get comfortable talking around her.

"I once thought about asking him for help with this girl I had a crush on, but I didn't because, you know, I don't talk," Owen said. "That made the asking part difficult. This was back in, like, eighth grade."

"Ooh! What girl?" I asked.

Owen blotched up about halfway but then took a sip of his soda. "I'll take that information with me to the grave."

"I'll get it out of you somehow," I said, narrowing my eyes.

"Doubtful," Owen said, shifting in his seat and leaning his elbows on the table.

"I don't know. I'm not a person who gives up too easily," I said. "Was it Grace Ricardo? Kyla Danning?"

"Glossies? Quinn. Give me a little credit," Owen said.

For some reason that made me blush. "Okay, Cora Impenna. Andrea Matteus?"

"Andrea Matteus is pure evil," Owen said. "She once spit a gummy bear into my snack pack. I could never love a person like that."

"All right, fine. Was it Kerri? Or Janice? I bet it was Janice. You guys used to play together when you were little, didn't you?"

"It wasn't Janice," he said. "Are you giving up yet?"

"Never!" I laughed. "Well, if you won't tell me who it was, at least tell me what ever happened with her."

Owen looked down at the table. "Nothing. I . . . I had this note I was going to give her, but I chickened out."

"Oh! That's so sweet. Sad but sweet," I said. "Come on. Who was it?"

"Why did I bring this up?" Owen said, reddening a bit. "What if I offer to help with the skit? Can we drop this, then?"

"Maybe," I replied, still dying of curiosity.

"Good. What can I do?" Owen asked, wiping his hands on one of the flimsy napkins. "Behind the scenes, of course."

"What? Can't convince you to put on a robe and wings and flit around the stage?" I asked, raising my eyebrows.

"Not unless you want to fight me," Owen said. "And trust me, I'm quicker than I look."

"I believe it," I replied. "But I'm pretty scrappy myself."

"I've heard that about you," Owen said, his eyes dancing.

"Really?"

"No."

I crumpled my napkin and threw it at him as he laughed. This was going way better than I'd imagined. I was even starting to see, for the first time, how he and Drew managed to be friends. I guess once Owen opened up to someone, he really became comfortable.

Owen took a sip of his soda, looked at me out of the corner of his eye, and flashed that incredible smile. My stomach grew warm, my heart skipped at least five beats, and suddenly all I could think about was kissing him. It was going to be perfect—I just knew it. I had definitely made the right choice.

"So, what're you doing tonight?" I asked Owen as he turned his car onto my street. The anticipation was killing me. I wasn't even sure how I was making conversation through all the tingling excitement.

"Homework. Again. Can you believe how much they're giving us?" he said. "I thought *junior* year was supposed to be the hard one."

"I know. I think it's because they know that we're going

to stop working as soon as our applications go out," I said. "They want to get in as much as possible before we go comatose."

Owen laughed, and it made me even more giddy. He stopped in front of my house and left the engine running.

"So," I said.

"So . . ." he replied. He gazed at me for a moment, but then he realized I was gazing back and turned away. "This was fun."

*All right, that's it,* I thought. Clearly I was going to have to take charge.

"Owen?"

"Yeah?" he said, looking at me.

Before he could blink or flinch, I leaned forward and planted my lips on his. He went all rigid, and my nerves went spastic. Oh, God! He hates it. He hates *me!* What am I doing?

But then, finally, he put his hands on my back, and his lips moved. Slightly. Taking this as a good sign, I opened my lips a little bit.

Nothing happened. If possible he froze up even more.

*Okay, this is embarrassing,* I thought. I took the hint and pulled away. He did hate me. He wanted to have nothing to do with me. My three-man-plan had just taken a horrible turn. I was about to beat a hasty retreat and bury myself in a bag of Oreos, when I saw Owen's face.

He was absolutely beaming. I swear, he looked so doofily happy, you would have thought we had just lost our virginity.

And suddenly I was grinning. How adorable could he be? Maybe Kerri was right. Maybe I *had* found the one person at Garden Hills High with less experience than me. We had just had an incredible afternoon, chatting and joking and laughing our butts off. I couldn't let one bad kiss—which *he* definitely didn't think was bad—ruin it for me. We'd just have to try it again sometime.

"Well, I guess I should go," I said.

"Okay. I'll . . . I'll e-mail you later," Owen said.

"Cool," I replied. "Thanks for the pizza."

Owen nodded, still smiling, and I climbed out of the car and ran inside. I called Kerri the second I got through the door.

"So, Owen the Gentleman, huh?" she said by way of greeting.

"How did you know?" I asked, tromping up the stairs.

"Saw you guys leaving school," she replied. "So, spill. Where'd you guys go?"

"Tino's."

"Geez, Quinn. Get a new routine! You keep bringing different guys in there, Tino might start thinking you're a slut," Kerri joked.

"I'll never be a slut with Owen," I told her, flopping down on top of my messy bed. "We just kissed, and he wouldn't even open his mouth."

"Aw! He's so virginal!" Kerri trilled.

"I know! And I really want to kiss him. Like *really* kiss him," I complained.

"Look at you! One night in the closet with Max

Eastwood, and all of a sudden you're dying for it!" Kerri teased.

"Ha-ha," I replied. "What am I going to do?"

"He'll come around eventually," Kerri said. "Hey! Maybe you can be the first girl to corrupt Owen Meyer!"

I laughed and flushed. The last thing I was capable of was corrupting anybody. But I kind of liked the possibility.

That night I was researching a paper for my U.S. history class when I saw Corey pop up on my buddy list. My heart seized up in my chest, and I almost signed off. Queen of avoidance. But before I could, an IM from him appeared on the screen.

El_Presidente: Hey, Donny . . .
Sk8_Quinn: hi
El_Presidente: Whaddup?

Okay. I could either act like nothing was going on or just bite the bullet and tell him. I figured this IM thing was better than face-to-face. Bless the person who'd created this super-impersonal mode of communication!

Sk8_Quinn: wanted 2 talk 2 U this afternoon. about owen.
El_Presidente: u guys together?
Sk8_Quinn: kind of . . .
El_Presidente: It's cool. Actually wanted to talk 2 U 2. about Elena.

Squirm time. What about Elena? Hadn't he just told me he didn't *want* Elena? What the heck was going on?

Oh. But wait a minute. It didn't matter, right? I had chosen Owen. I took a deep breath and typed back.

Sk8_Quinn: u 2 back 2gether?
El_Presidente: yeah. she broke up w/ logan. she was just here. long talk. but good!
Sk8_Quinn: oh. that's nice.

Ugh! Ugh! Ugh! It killed me that Elena could just snap her fingers and Corey would go right back to her. So annoying! He deserved so much better.

But honestly? I was also relieved.

Looked like not choosing Corey was the right way to go. What if I had put myself out there, and he had gone back to Elena anyway? Well, let's just say it wouldn't have been pretty and would probably have involved my curling up in a fetal position in one of the darkest corners of my house for an entire weekend.

Phew.

I wished him and his girlfriend luck, and I signed off.

I guess I'd deal with Max at school.

# nine

"So, now that you're dating my best friend, do I get free ice cream?" Kerri asked Owen in the hallway the following morning.

He turned his ten specific shades of red and purple and trained his eyes at the floor. I wished he could come out of his shell around other people the way he had around me. He was so funny. If people knew that about him, they would *love* him. Of course, people had been telling me similar things for years, so I was not one to judge. Instead, I shot Kerri a look of death for putting him on the spot. But then, that was Kerri. If Owen was going to hang out with me, he was going to hang out with her, and he would have to get used to being put on the spot. Believe me.

"I'll buy you some ice cream, baby," Drew said,

clucking his tongue and looking Kerri up and down.

"Drew!" Owen said.

Apparently I was going to have to get used to Drew. Fun, fun, fun.

"In your dreams, Spencer," Kerri said.

"I am a firm believer that dreams can come true," Drew said, raising an arm and leaning against the wall near Owen's locker as if he was posing for a fashion photographer.

Kerri rolled her eyes. I was surprised. Rarely, if ever, did she give up a chance for a comeback.

"You get free ice cream anyway since you work there," Owen reminded her.

"Oh, right," she said. "Free fries, then?"

"I could buy you fries, too," Drew offered.

Kerri and I exchanged a glance and laughed at the ridiculousness of this conversation. Owen paused in front of his locker and started in on his combination. I had a feeling he was relieved to have something to distract him.

"So . . . Quinn. I have to work most days this week, but if you want to come by . . ."

He let the invitation linger there as he dug into his locker. I wasn't sure if he really wanted to hang out with me or if he was just giving me an obligatory invite. I glanced at Kerri for guidance. She just widened her eyes and tilted her head toward Owen.

What did *that* mean?

"Uh . . . okay. Sure," I said. "But only if *I* can get free fries," I added lamely.

Owen smiled. "You can get free anything."

"That's my boy-*eee!*" Drew cried, slapping Owen on the back and kneading his shoulders like he was a prize fighter.

I ignored Drew as my heart warmed. It was kind of cool that I could put that look on Owen's face. Behind the guys Kerri fake gagged. I whacked her arm.

"Okay. I'll . . . uh . . . see you later," Owen said, shoving some books into his bag and zipping it up.

"Yeah. Cool," I replied.

"Cool."

Drew hovered behind him expectantly. Owen looked at the wall, at Kerri, at the floor, and at the locker. He touched the locker door with his fingertips, tightened his bag strap, shoved his hand into his pocket, and shifted his weight. It was like watching a mime show. A painful one. And then, out of nowhere, he pecked me quickly and awkwardly on the cheek, turned, and jogged past Drew down the hall.

"He's all grown up!" Drew announced gleefully, thrusting his arms into the air. "He's all grown up and he's all grown up and he's all grown up!"

Someone had seen *Swingers* one too many times.

"You are such a loser," Kerri said with her patented look of disdain.

"You so want me," Drew replied. He backed up, holding his arms wide. "Just make sure you don't wait too long, cuz you never know how long prime stud like this is gonna stay on the market."

He turned and loped off after Owen.

"Well past the expiration date, I'm sure!" Kerri shouted after him.

I laughed and touched my cheek.

"Wow. That was some kiss," Kerri said. "I think we just regressed to fifth grade."

"Shut up. It's sweet," I said as we moved down the hall.

"Yeah! Kind of like hanging out with him at the Snack Shack while he works. Very romantic," Kerri said.

"Don't judge," I told her. "This whole thing was your idea, remember? Besides, I like him."

"Uh-oh. Incoming," Kerri said.

Sure enough, Max Eastwood was trudging down the hall toward us. He was moving so quickly that underclassmen of all shapes and sizes were dodging out of his way to keep from being trampled. My heart seized up. This could be bad.

"Quinn," he said, stopping in front of us. "I have to ask you something."

"Okay," I replied. His face was a dark shade of red, and his breath was short and shallow. He looked set to pop.

"What's up with you and that Owen guy?" he asked.

I glanced at Kerri. She stepped closer to me.

"We're . . . uh . . . going out," I told him.

"What!?" he shouted, throwing his hands up and letting them slap down at his sides. "I thought *we* were going out! You're cheating on me already?"

Kerri snorted a laugh and hid it with a cough. I started to slowly burn as a crowd began to form.

"We went out once," I said. "We weren't *going out*."

He looked like I had just started speaking Spanish. Backward. "What? Why not?" he asked. "Why him and not me?"

"Well . . . um . . . I think you just got a little too close too fast," I said, backing up a step.

Max looked up at the ceiling and groaned, curling his hands into fists. "Why do girls always say this to me?" he half-whimpered.

Another snort-laugh-cough from Kerri.

"I'm really sorry, Max," I said.

"Whatever," he replied.

He let out a long breath, curled his broad shoulders forward, and loped off down the hall with his head hanging.

"Wow," Kerri said as our spectators dispersed with a grumble at the relatively low drama content. "I thought you were a total freak for not picking him, but now I get it. *He's* the freak."

I sighed. "Apparently."

"Is it always this dead around here?" I asked Owen as I rearranged my cards. I had pulled a stool up to the counter at the Snack Shack to sit across from Owen by the window. He was teaching me to play rummy while about a dozen kids messed around in the water. Aside from their parents, a couple of die-hard sunbathers, and the lifeguards, The Mill was deserted.

"On cool days, yeah," he said, glancing at the clock. "They should really close at the end of August, but I think Marty is an 'endless summer' guy."

Marty was the proprietor of The Mill—one of those guys who had an almost orange tan year-round and was always wearing tank tops and shorts that were way too short for his sixty-plus bod. A lot of people thought it was weird that he kept The Mill open through September, but even though there were a few cool days in there, most of them were still wicked hot and I, for one, was always happy to still be able to swim on the weekends or after school. Besides, as Marty pointed out at the end-of-summer bash every August, summer didn't *actually* end until September 21.

"True," I said. I looked at my cards and at the discard pile. "So, I can pick that one up if I need it?" I asked.

"Yeah, but you have to put another down," he told me.

"'Kay."

I picked up and put down and then it was Owen's turn. *Some date,* I heard Kerri say in my head. *What are you guys? Geriatric?* I shook my head slightly and tried to clear my disloyal thoughts. It was nice that Owen was making time for me even though he was busy. And this was fun. I liked games of all kinds.

Even old-people card games.

Owen made his move and a sharp whistle blared off to my right. I turned to see Josh Marx standing up in his life-guard chair, shouting at a couple of kids who were shoving each other around near the high dive.

"No pushing!" he yelled. "If I have to warn you one more time, you guys are outta here!"

The two kids sprang apart, and one of them sheepishly

held his hands behind his back. I watched Josh as he sat down again with a smirk on. Damn, he looked good all shirtless and tan and in charge.

"Quinn?" Owen said. "It's your turn."

"Oh. Sorry," I said, pulling myself back to the game. I snagged the ten of clubs he'd discarded and used it to make a four of a kind, slapping it down in front of me. Then I discarded another card.

"Wow. You're really getting good at this," he said. "You sure you're not a ringer? Because scamming a guy on a third date is not cool."

I smiled coyly. "I'm a quick study."

"I'll have to remember that," Owen said flirtatiously.

My heart fluttered and I smiled back, not really sure what he meant but glad he was flirting. Maybe sometime today we could get around to trying that kiss again. If only we could get that right, we could—

Another whistle caught my attention. I glanced over my shoulder at Josh. There was something about that point where his shoulder muscle met his biceps. I just wanted to grab that part of his arm. Just once. Just—

"Quinn."

I blushed. Hard. Had Owen caught me drooling?

"Sorry," I said again. "Hang on."

Enough was enough. I was supposed to be over Josh Marx. I was here for Owen. I climbed down, turned my stool around, and sat down again. Now if I wanted to gape at him, I would have to break my neck to do it.

"Sun was in my eyes," I explained. I picked up a card

150

from the deck and grinned. "Rummy!" I discarded and put down my straight to finish out my hand.

Owen groaned. "This is embarrassing," he said.

"Aw! Want me to throw the next game?" I teased.

Owen narrowed his eyes. "Just for that I'm gonna take you down," he said, gathering up the cards to shuffle them.

Josh's whistle blared again, and all my muscles tensed, but I did not turn around. I was doing a lot of things I had never done before. Including getting a life.

"You in?" Owen asked, shuffling.

I smiled resolutely. "Definitely."

# ten

The movie theater was dark and cool. The back row was secluded, and the new seats were cushy and comfy. The popcorn bucket was balanced on my legs and every time Owen went to grab a handful, his knee rubbed against mine. I could feel him breathing in the darkness. Whenever he laughed, I smiled. I had absolutely no idea what was going on in the stupid buddy comedy playing on the screen. All I could think about was what would happen next. What would happen when we left the theater and he drove me home? Would he kiss me for real this time? This was, after all, our fourth date.

Well, if playing rummy at his job in full view of my ex-crush and a few dozen other people could be considered a date.

The movie was mercifully short, and soon enough we were back in his car, headed for my house. He stopped right in front of the walkway to my front door and put the car in park.

"So . . ." he said.

I think if someone were to do a study, they would find that this was Owen's most-used word.

"Funny movie," I said. Though I couldn't even recall the plot.

"Yeah," he replied. "If you're a twelve-year-old."

"I heard you laughing a lot," I told him.

"Well, I'm a twelve-year-old at heart," he said.

I smiled, slid a little closer to the parking brake, and looked at him. His knuckles went white on the steering wheel. Was I being too obvious, or not obvious enough? I mean, I thought all teenage boys were nothing but a steaming pressure cooker of bubbling hormones. Why wouldn't he even *look* at me?

Then, out of nowhere, he released the wheel and grabbed me. One hand went around the back of my neck, the other to my shoulder. I felt like he was grabbing a side of beef. Or maybe a tuba.

"I—"

Suddenly his lips were pressed against mine, all dry and hard and flat.

*Okay, don't panic,* I told myself, my eyes wide. *Just . . . try to move or something.*

I shifted slightly, thinking I could wrap my arms around him and direct somehow. I almost started laughing

153

at the very idea that I would be directing anyone when it came to kissing, but it really did seem that I knew what I was doing compared to Owen. But when he felt me move, he immediately pulled away.

"Sorry," he said.

*What?*

"No! I—I was just getting comfortable," I said. "I wasn't backing off."

"Oh," Owen said.

Even in the dark I could tell his face was developing its topographical blotch map. I didn't understand. I liked him so much. And I was pretty sure he liked me. Why couldn't we get this right? *Why?* We had so much chemistry when we were just hanging out and talking. Why did we both become awkward idiots when we tried to kiss?

"Owen," I said, figuring we could talk about this. Maybe we could be mature and get past the awkwardness somehow. We had actually gotten *good* at talking lately.

He glanced at me, his expression pained, and I realized I was insane. Talking about something this loaded and important? Me? Him? We were the poster children for avoidance.

So instead I grabbed him and kissed him again. Owen's entire body went stiff with surprise, and he leaned back, so I was practically on top of him. Suddenly I felt like I was committing sexual assault. I pulled away—and jammed an elbow into his gut while trying to regain my balance.

Owen let out an *"oof,"* and I flushed with humiliation.

"'Kay. I'd better go," I said, trying to sound normal.

Instead I sounded like I was on the verge of tears. I fumbled for the door handle, thanked him for the movie and popcorn, and ran into the house.

I had no idea what to expect the next day in school, but Owen acted totally normal, as if nothing odd had happened. Maybe I could redeem myself. Maybe if we kept trying, eventually we would get around to having a good kiss. If there was one thing Quinn Donohue was not, it was a quitter.

So that weekend I found myself, once again, hanging at The Mill. Kerri had the day off, so she came along to loaf around in the sand and throw her freedom in her co-workers' faces, and Janice joined us as well. It was a sweltering September day and unlike earlier in the week The Mill was slammed. I found Owen behind the counter of the Snack Shack, all harried and hassled by a line of impatient, ice cream–hungry kiddies.

"Sorry," he said, lifting his baseball cap to wipe the sweat off with the back of his hand. "I'm not going to be able to hang out much. Can I catch up with you on my break?"

"Sure. No problem," I told him. "We'll find a spot near the water."

Kerri, Janice, and I walked around to the deep section, where couples and adult groups usually hung out. We laid our towels near the edge of the water. Janice pulled out a novel and buried her nose in it.

"So, you guys gotten nasty yet?" Kerri asked as she

sprawled out on her stomach.

"Whoa. No preamble or anything, huh?" Janice asked.

"Seriously." I scoffed. "Yes, Kerri. He came over last night and gave it to me hard all night long. I just forgot to tell you about it."

"Still nothing, huh?" she asked.

"*Nada*. Zilch. Zero," I said. I sat down on my towel and leaned back on my elbows. "Are there chastity belts for the mouth? Cuz his lips do not open."

"Okay, ew," Janice said. Did I mention she can be kind of a prude? She pulled out her iPod and plugged herself in.

"I think we offended her," I whispered.

"Love the girl, but offending her is easy to do," Kerri said with a smile. "So what the heck is up with Owen? Most guys would have been trying to round third by now."

Across the pond, Josh Marx climbed down from his lifeguard chair as another guard took over. I ignored the extra pound my heart gave when I realized he was coming our way.

"I guess I should just be patient," I said, my eyes trained on Josh. "I mean, it's not like I'm in some big rush, right?"

"You should be," Kerri said. "You've wasted half your prime years already."

"Ha-ha," I said.

And then Josh was there, and he was pausing by our towels. His head blocked the sun, and he looked like some kind of golden god, all oiled and sun kissed. Too bad I didn't like him anymore.

"Ladies," he said.

Kerri squinted up at him, rolled her eyes, and turned her head away on the towel. Janice noticed his shadow and turned up the volume on her iPod.

"Hi," I replied.

"So, I'm off duty now. You girls going in?" he asked.

My stomach flip-flopped, and I looked at Kerri. She simply took a deep breath and let it out audibly. What was her problem? Josh Marx was asking us to swim! Didn't she know this was one of many lifelong dreams come true?

Oh, but wait. I was supposed to be ignoring him. It was a big part of the get-over-him plan.

I glanced at Josh again, smiling down at me. Screw the get-over-him plan. It wasn't working.

"Ker?" I said.

"You guys go," she said. Then she whacked Janice's leg. Janice pulled one bud from one ear. "I think I'm going to go get a soda. At the *Snack Shack*," she added pointedly.

I swallowed the lump of guilt in my throat.

"Want to come?" she asked Janice.

"Sure," Janice said with a shrug.

They both stood and grabbed their wallets. I wished Kerri wouldn't make such a big deal. It was just a swim. And Owen was too busy to hang out anyway.

"I'm in," I said to Josh, standing and stepping self-consciously out of my shorts.

"Cool," Josh said, looking past me at Kerri and Janice. "Soda can't wait?"

"Sorry," Kerri said with a shrug. Then she shot me a

look before sauntering off toward the long line, Janice scurrying to stay in step with her.

The water was freezing. We had been through a couple of cool nights, and The Mill couldn't recover during the day no matter how sunny and blistering it was. I tried to stop my teeth from chattering as Josh and I hung from the platform in the middle of the deep section.

"So, you and Owen Meyer, huh?" he said. "How's that going?"

"Fine. Great," I lied. *Why? Why are you asking? Why do you want to know?*

"Really?"

He seemed surprised.

"What?" I said.

"Well, it just makes zero sense," he said.

Hadn't he said something similar about me and Max at Stoller's party? Was there anyone in Garden Hills that Josh thought I could date, or did he just think of me as a sexless wonder? I was starting to get all irritated, but then he turned and grabbed the ladder, climbing up onto the platform. His bathing suit clung to his legs as he climbed, perfectly outlining his ass. The anger melted away.

"Why does it make zero sense?" I asked, following him up.

Josh walked out onto the diving board and bounced a couple of times on the end, facing me. "Because he's totally lame and boring," he said with a grin. Then he backflipped off the diving board and disappeared under the water.

Okay, that was mean. But suddenly I couldn't stop smiling—my cold, clammy cheeks stretching painfully. I mean, it was a compliment, right? He meant that Owen and I didn't make sense because I was *not* lame and boring. At least I hoped that was what he was trying to say.

I climbed onto the diving board with shaky legs and did a safe dive so as not to flub and crack my head open in my giddiness. Josh was waiting for me in the water. I was hoping he would elaborate. Maybe tell me how very unlame and unboring I was. We swam back toward the shore.

"What's up with Kerri?" he asked me.

Damn it. Subject change.

"What do you mean?" I asked.

"She's kind of a buzz kill."

"No she's not," I said.

"Well, she hates me," he said. "We worked together all summer and she barely said two words to me."

I had no idea what to say to this. As far as I knew, Kerri had no strong feelings one way or the other for Josh. If she had come off as negative while they were guarding, it was probably because of me—because I had been pining for so long and he had been ignoring me for so long. Of course, all of that seemed to be changing now.

"She doesn't hate you," I said finally. Just to make him feel better. And, also, if he was developing an interest in me, I didn't want him staying away because my best friend supposedly despised him.

"Whatever," Josh said, lifting one shoulder. "I just

figured I'd ask, since we're doing the Spirit Show together. You know. Don't need any *Behind the Music* drama."

"Well, she's cool. Don't worry," I said, impressed at his professionalism.

"Cool," he said with a heart-stopping smile. "Hey. Check it out." He lifted his chin toward the Snack Shack, and I turned around. There was nothing there but the usual line of customers.

"What?"

Before the syllable was fully out of my mouth, Josh had dunked me.

I nearly choked from laughing as our legs got tangled up under the water. I slipped out of his grasp, surfaced, and reached for his head. He ducked out of the way, but I managed to grab his arm, pull myself up, and get my hands on his shoulders. He struggled, but I used every ounce of my strength and pushed him down. Under the water he turned and grabbed me around the waist. When he came up again, he stood up and threw me. I heard myself shriek and realized that I probably looked like a huge dork, but I didn't care.

"You're going down!" I shouted.

"You'll have to catch me first!" he replied, taking off.

I splashed him hard and raced after him. Somewhere in the distance I heard a whistle blow, and I dimly recognized that this kind of roughhousing was against Mill rules, but so what? I was in the middle of a dunking fight and splash war with Josh Marx. Laughing. Touching. Wrestling.

The rules were pretty much the last thing I cared about.

# eleven

That evening I stared at my wall, seeing nothing but Josh's face. Josh's grin as he splashed me. His openmouthed laugh as he tried to dunk me. His sympathetic smile as he helped my drowned-rat self out of the pond. He'd held my hands—both of them—as he pulled me out of the water, then wrapped an arm around my shoulders as we tripped, exhausted and laughing, back to my towel.

I shivered happily. Every single time I thought about it, I shivered happily. I was shivering a lot.

"Dinner's ready!" my mom shouted from downstairs.

I almost fell off my bed. Inhaling, I realized the whole house smelled like her spaghetti sauce, and my stomach grumbled. How had I not noticed that before?

*Because you were in la-la land with Josh,* I thought.

And suddenly I was irritated with myself. I had let Josh Marx reinfiltrate my psyche. He had taken over yet again. After I had promised myself—not to mention Kerri—that I was done with his slutty self. Could I be any weaker?

Meanwhile, Owen was out there somewhere thinking I was his closed-mouth-kissing girlfriend, and I hadn't even defended him when Josh had called him boring. And, of course, the ultimate irony was that if I wasn't "with" Owen, I never would have been at The Mill today and I never would have gone swimming with Josh in the first place. I loathed myself.

"I'll be right down!" I shouted to my mother.

I grabbed my cell and dialed Owen. He picked up on the first ring.

"Hello?"

"Hey, Owen, it's Quinn," I said.

"Hi!" he replied, sounding very happy to hear my voice.

"Listen, I was wondering if you wanted to do something tomorrow," I offered. What, I had no idea.

"Actually, I'm working a double tomorrow—open to close," Owen replied. "But you can come by, if you want."

I held my breath to keep from groaning. Sitting around while Owen served ice cream was about the last thing I wanted to do with my Sunday. It was okay once or twice, but did he really think it was entertaining for me to hang out at his workplace all the time? Were we ever going to do anything else?

*Maybe he* is *lame and boring,* a little voice in my head suggested. But I knew this wasn't true, and I instantly felt guilty for thinking it. Not guilty enough, though.

"Actually, I think I'll hit the skate park," I told him. "But I'll talk to you tomorrow night."

"Oh. Okay. Cool," Owen said.

He sounded disappointed and my guilt doubled. I was relieved when my mom called up to me again. It was the perfect excuse to get off the phone as quickly as possible.

I hit the skate park bright and early the next morning. Well, early for boarders, which is anytime before noon. There's a whole different crowd there in the morning—younger kids who are just starting out and guys my age who don't know what they're doing and are afraid of being mocked when the seasoned boarders show up. There's even this one old guy, Bart, who has to be like fifty, but he can shred with the best of them. He comes in the mornings because he works afternoons at the local Blockbuster. I'm not kidding.

I did a couple of runs through all the ramps, taking it easy and getting my blood pumping. It was one of the first cool mornings of the season, and I liked feeling my body temperature rise and push away the goose bumps on my skin. It was exhilarating and relaxing all at once. I smiled as I hit the big ramp, happy I had decided to go my own way instead of hovering around Owen all day.

I was descending the slope when I saw another boarder coming down the other side. I almost lost my balance when I realized it was Josh, but I managed not to deck and make an idiot of myself. He grinned and waved as we zoomed past each other at the bottom of the bowl. My heart pounded when we hit the opposite crests in exact unison, then dove back down and slid by each other again. It was like we were in perfect sync.

*What's he doing here?* I thought, grabbing the lip of my board and flipping around. Josh hadn't been seen at the park since school started—probably too busy with football and homework and girls. I couldn't help wondering if he was here because of me. I mean, one day we have a huge flirt-fest at The Mill, and the next he shows up at my number-one hangout. Coincidence? I think not.

Josh stood at the top of the ramp as I ascended again. I popped up next to him and stopped. My chest was heaving up and down, both from his presence and from the physical exertion.

"What's up?" Josh said, sitting down on the lip of the ramp.

"Not much," I replied. I was sweating profusely, and I hoped I didn't smell. I couldn't remember if I'd put on deodorant. Just in case, I sat a good foot away from him. "What are you doing here?"

Josh shrugged. "Felt like a workout."

I nodded and stared across the park to the flattop where a couple of kids were trying out their new boards.

"Actually, that's a lie," Josh said with a laugh. "I figured you'd be here. That's why I came."

*No way. No way, no way, no way.*

"Yeah?" I said. I felt like I could vomit a little bit.

He nodded and looked at me. "Yeah."

Somehow I met his gaze. It was as if the entire world

had stopped and all that was left was him and me and the foot of space between us. This wasn't happening. This couldn't possibly be happening.

"The thing is . . . I can't believe I'm gonna say this," Josh began. "But I always kind of thought you liked me."

Snagged! "Oh . . . I . . . ." How the hell do you respond to that?

"But then you started going out with that tool Owen Meyer. . . ."

"We've only been out a couple of times," I blurted. Then I realized how pathetic that sounded, and I added, "And he's not a tool. I . . . I like him."

Even though my breath was growing short. Even though every inch of me was dying to kiss Josh. Even though there were distinct signs that he was interested in me, finally, after all this time, I still felt the need to defend Owen.

"Of course you do. He can get you all kinds of free ice cream," Josh said.

I laughed in an embarrassed, on-the-spot, holy-crap-I-can't-believe-this-is-happening kind of way.

"But I can give you this," Josh said.

And then he was kissing me. I have no idea how he closed the space between us. All I knew was that I had never been kissed like this in my life, even by Corey or Max. Josh's lips moved over mine, pressing, searching. He parted my lips without hesitation, and my whole body responded. I slid closer to him, smiling even as I kissed him back. He touched my face gently with his fingers and held my back firmly with his other hand, like all he wanted was to be closer to me. We might have kissed for five minutes or five seconds—I had no idea. It was that mind blowing.

Josh Marx *was* everything I'd thought he would be. The dream had actually come true.

"He what? He *what?*" Kerri shouted, standing in the doorway of her house in her baby doll pajamas. "He did not!"

"He did! He kissed me!" I was beaming so hard, I could have subbed for the spotlight at the Spirit Show. "A lot."

"Get in here!" Kerri cried, practically yanking my arm out of its socket.

"Kerri! Who's at the door?" Kerri's father called from the back of the house.

"It's Quinn, Dad!" she shouted back impatiently.

"Oh! Does she want pancakes?" he asked.

"No, she does not want pancakes!" Kerri shouted, yanking me into the family room, where her two little sisters were watching SpongeBob SquarePants with plates of pancakes and bacon on their laps.

"Actually, I am kind of hungry," I said, eyeing the girls' food.

"Later," Kerri said, shoving me down onto the piano bench. "How was it?"

I grinned. I was so happy that she was excited. Considering her opinions on Josh, I had been afraid she was going to smack me upside the head and tell me to snap out of it. Besides, I had broken the number-one rule of her whole three-man-plan.

"It was perfection," I told her. "Remember how gaga I was about Max? Well add about fifty more ga's."

"You're kidding," she said. "Wow. Josh Marx. You finally landed Josh Marx."

"I know," I said, and we both stared off into space. "I can't believe it."

We sat there for a second, lost in our own thoughts. In the background SpongeBob and Patrick argued about jellyfish.

"You're not mad at me?" I asked finally.

"Why would I be mad?" Kerri asked, her brow knitting.

"Well, I know you're not a big Josh Marx fan—"

"I will be if you start dating him," she said.

"And this kind of kills your whole plan," I added.

Kerri clucked her tongue. "Please, the whole idea was to get you a date. And we definitely accomplished that. And then some. Do you realize you've kissed four guys in the last two weeks? You're such a little ho!"

"Kerri!" I said, glancing at her sisters.

"Please. They're mesmerized," she said.

In fact, they didn't seem to be blinking or moving, other than to blindly shovel pancakes into their mouths.

"Holy crap, I don't believe it," Kerri said suddenly. And from her tone I knew she'd just had a new revelation.

"What?"

"He is such a *guy!* You do know why he kissed you now, after all this time, don't you?" Kerri said.

"Actually, I have no idea."

"He's jealous! He saw you with Max. He saw you with

Corey. Then you're dating Owen. He just wanted to prove he could still get you!" Kerri announced.

Suddenly my heart felt hard and cold. "So, you're saying he doesn't actually like me?"

Kerri's face went flat. "No. I'm not saying that. I'm not saying that at all," she said. "I'm just saying that that's why he woke up and smelled the hottie."

Oh, God. Maybe this was a bad thing. Maybe this meant that once he *got* me, he would get bored with me. Well, then, I would just have to make sure he didn't. I forced myself to see the glass as half full. This was not going to ruin the best day of my life.

"I should have thought of dating other guys a long time ago," I said.

Kerri winced. "Speaking of other guys, what're you gonna do?"

My shoulders slumped. I'd known this question was coming. "I have no idea."

"Well, you have to tell Owen," she said.

Ugh! The very thought was totally depressing. Maybe this was why I didn't date. Dating meant dealing with— *eek!*—emotions. Even worse, *other people's* emotions. "I know," I said finally. "I can't pass up the chance at Josh Marx, right?"

"Especially not for a guy who hasn't even slipped you the tongue," Kerri agreed.

I snorted a lackluster laugh. "Poor Owen," I said.

Kerri placed an arm around my shoulders. "Welcome to your love life."

# twelve

"I just don't think it's gonna work out," I said, staring at Owen's sneakers.

We were standing in a corner of the cafeteria, and when I glanced up at him he literally looked cornered. He gripped a strap on his backpack with a white-knuckled hand and shifted his weight from foot to foot, also staring at the floor. The blotches were out of control.

"Owen?" My heart felt like it had been squeezed down to the size of an acorn, and I was sweating like a marathoner. I just wanted this to be over.

"Yeah?" he said.

"Are you okay?" I asked.

"Yeah, sure," he said.

Though he looked anything but. I wanted him to crack

a joke. To say something self-deprecating. Or even something me-deprecating. To let me know that he didn't hate me. But I guess in breaking up with him I had turned him back into the old Owen. The one who couldn't talk to me. It sucked.

"I just think we feel more like friends, you know?" I said.

I wanted him to agree with me. I wanted him to say he felt the same way. That he knew this was going nowhere. Instead he looked like he was going to cry.

"Yeah, sure," he said. "Okay."

"Okay, then," I said, attempting to swallow.

What was I supposed to do? Kiss him and walk away? No. That seemed weird for two people who barely even touched when they *were* dating. I felt rooted to the spot and at the same time I felt that if I didn't get out of there now one of us was going to have an aneurysm.

"Well, see ya," I said finally.

"Yeah. Okay," he said. He only had three words left in his vocabulary. "Bye."

I turned and walked as fast as possible to my table, where Kerri, Lindsey, and Janice were already eating their lunches. I sighed and collapsed into a chair, my head thumping onto my arms on the table.

"Was it bad?" Kerri asked.

"Epically," I replied.

"Well, at least it's over," Lindsey said.

"Or not," Janice added, glancing over my shoulder.

My heart dropped when I turned around. Drew was

stalking toward us all gangsta-like, a look of pure hatred on his face. Back at his table Owen's head hung, and I could tell he was trying to become invisible. I knew he was as miserable as I was that Drew was about to make a scene.

"So, what? You suddenly too good for my boy?" Drew asked, landing at the head of our table. "Who the hell do you think you are, beyotch?"

That's exactly how he said it—be-yotch. My skin was melting a hole in the plastic chair.

"Back off, Spencer," Kerri said.

"What are you, the bodyguard?" Drew snapped, taking a defensive stance. "I'll take you on right now."

"Leave her alone. It just didn't work out, okay?" Kerri said.

Drew looked at me and narrowed his eyes. Then a lightbulb seemed to pop on over his head. He grinned, crossed his arms over his chest, and looked at Kerri.

"I'll leave her alone if you go out with me," he said.

"Not a chance!" I blurted.

"Excuse me, Jezebel, but I don't believe I was talking to you," Drew said. All of our jaws dropped. "There's an offer on the table," he said to Kerri. "You go out with me once, and I leave her alone. Otherwise I humiliate her every day for the rest of the year. And you know I never get bored."

Kerri looked at me. I tried to convey solidarity, but I have a feeling I just looked desperate. I knew what she was going to do before she even said it.

"Fine. I'll go out with you," she said.

"Yes!" Drew cheered, making a fist.

"But I pick the time and place," Kerri said.

"Fine by me," Drew replied as he rubbed his hands together. "You ladies enjoy your lunch."

He walked off with a cocky spring in his step that made me want to throw my skateboard at him.

"Are you insane?" Janice blurted. "Drew Spencer?"

"Seriously, Kerri. You didn't have to do that," I told her.

"Hey. I got you into this mess," she said with a shrug.

And that was when I knew, beyond a shadow of a doubt, that I had the best friend in the entire world.

Friday afternoon I stood in the wings of the auditorium, drunk with glory. Our version of "Beauty School Dropout" was bringing down the house. Josh looked hilarious in his pink wig and poodle skirt, and he was completely hamming it up, clutching his hands and batting his fake eyelashes at Kerri like she was the love of his life. Kerri sang her heart out, looking sexy in her white Elvis-inspired jumpsuit while twenty of the hottest guys in our class flitted around her in white robes and curlers, waving their arms and backing her up.

"You did it, Donny," Corey said, hooking an arm over my shoulders with a grin.

"We did it," I replied.

"Okay. We did it," he said.

I glanced out at the audience. The seniors and juniors in the front rows were actually doubled over. Mr. Pransky, my rotund physics teacher, was laughing so hard he was crying. I was in heaven.

172

At the end of the skit Rasheed Stevenson, the biggest linebacker on the football team, was lowered from the ceiling wearing wings and carrying a harp. It took eight of his fellow linemen to hold him there, but they did it, and we earned a standing ovation.

The moment the curtains went down, everyone started screaming and laughing and jumping up and down. Josh raced right off the stage and grabbed me up in his arms, spinning me around and hugging the air right out of me. But who needed oxygen at a time like this? We had *so* won! And Josh Marx was hugging me right there in front of everyone!

"You rock, Quinn Donohue!" Josh shouted. "If we don't win this, I'll shave my head. I'm not kidding."

I laughed as he placed me back on the floor. Then Kerri, who had to descend a ladder before she could join the festivities, ran over and hugged me as well.

"You guys were amazing," I said, gripping her, too.

"Thanks," Josh said with a grin. "So, listen, I'm having a party tomorrow night before the dance. You should come," he said to me. Then he glanced uncertainly at Kerri. "Both of you."

My heart warmed. He was reaching out to Kerri even though he thought she hated him. He must really like me.

And, okay, so it wasn't an invitation to the dance per se, but that meant I *had* to go to his party. As far as I knew he didn't have a date for homecoming yet. Maybe we would end up going from the party to the dance together. Anything was possible.

"What do you think?" I asked Kerri.

For a second she looked as if I had just put her on the spot, but I blinked, and the moment passed. "Sure," she said with a smile. "We'll be there."

"Cool," Josh said.

Then he turned, let out a whoop, and started the triumphant cheering all over again. Corey whipped out a bottle of sparkling cider, shook it up, and sprayed everyone with it.

At that moment I knew nothing could bring me down.

"Aw, yeah! We ready to party?" Drew Spencer shouted as we walked into Josh's house on Saturday afternoon.

He handed his plastic-wrapped suit to Josh and was already dancing—not that there was any music—on his way into the living room.

"What's he doing here?" Josh asked, confused.

"He's my date," Kerri said flatly, handing over her dress in its garment bag.

Josh shrugged as Kerri passed him by, and then he grinned at me. "Glad you guys could come."

"Me, too," I said, folding my own dress over my arm.

I couldn't believe I was in Josh Marx's house. It was one of a few modern homes on the outskirts of town, and it seemed as if everything in it belonged in a museum. All the walls were white, and the few pieces of art on the walls had those little spotlights suspended over them. There wasn't a mark on any of the walls, unlike my house where finger-prints and scratches prevailed. The smell of lemon-scented

Lysol added to the antiseptic vibe. Somehow I couldn't imagine that Josh's parents approved of his having half the senior class over for beer and chips if this was how they kept their house.

"Here. We're putting the clothes in my mom's closet," Josh said, leading me upstairs. His party fell right between the football game and the dance, so we were all supposed to get ready here. "My dad moved out last month, so his half of the closet is empty."

"Oh," I replied, following him up the steps. "Sorry."

"No, it's okay," Josh said, glancing over his shoulder. "He's kind of an ass."

I attempted a smile as we passed a few closed doors, behind one of which I could hear the obvious sounds of people fooling around. A couple of girls from my class smiled at Josh and held up their drinks. A couple sat on the floor making out, as if they were waiting for one of the rooms to free up. I felt more like I was in a brothel than someone's home, but Josh seemed unfazed.

He strolled into a humongous bedroom with a sign taped to the door that read OFF LIMITS! The bed was at least a king. It was perfectly made with a white bedspread and red and orange throw pillows. A bathroom with a Jacuzzi tub inside sat at the far end of the room, its double doors slid aside. Josh walked into an open closet about the size of my bedroom and hung Kerri's and Drew's things next to a bunch of other dresses and suits. I added mine to the collection. I had gone with a basic blue dress with spaghetti straps.

"Nice," Josh said, checking out my dress and nodding. "Can't wait to see you in it." I could have died of embarrassment and pleasure. "Come on. We'll get you a drink."

Downstairs, the living room was packed with people from my class sipping from red plastic cups, their voices echoing off the high ceilings. Some of the guys were messing around in the pool, visible through sliding glass doors to the backyard. Most of the girls stayed inside, probably to avoid getting thrown in and therefore being forced to shower again. The atmosphere was intense and excited, to say the least. The football team had actually won our big rivalry game, and all anyone could talk about in the stands was the seniors' Spirit Show skit. We were so going to win the contest at the dance that night. I just knew we were.

"Quinn Donohue! How does it feel to be a hero?" Leon Monroe shouted, emerging from the crowd and handing me a cup of punch. Leon was Josh's best friend and had been one of the biggest heroes of the game that afternoon.

"Take it all in," Josh said, looping an arm around my shoulders. "This is what they call 'your big moment.'"

I grinned and looked at his hand on my shoulder. Just then I couldn't have cared less about homecoming or the Spirit Show or anything else. It was my moment because Josh Marx had his arm around me.

Barf-worthy, I know. But I had been waiting for this since I was still in braces. The only way it could have been more perfect would have been if Josh had asked me to be his date for the dance, but it wasn't a big deal that he hadn't. I knew he didn't have a date. He knew I didn't have a date.

I figured we would probably be spending most of the night together. And if I could get a redux of that kiss-of-perfection, I would go to every dance solo for the rest of my life.

There was a scream and a splash in the backyard, and Josh flinched away from me.

"I'd better check out those losers before they do something stupid," he said.

Then he left me there alone with Leon and three other football players nursing their beers and cups of punch. Suddenly I felt beyond conspicuous. I had nothing to say to these people. But maybe I should at least try. After all, they were Josh's friends.

"So, good game today," I said.

"Try freakin' *awesome* game!" Trey Lasky said. They all slapped hands and downed half their beers.

"Dude! Did you see the way I nailed that safety?" Leon said to his friends. "He's still got snot bubbles coming out of his nose!"

Very pleasant.

"Aw, yeah, brotha!" Trey said, slapping his hand again, then slamming his chest into Leon's.

I glanced toward the back door, wondering when Josh was going to return. Not soon enough, I assumed.

"I . . . uh . . . I think I'm gonna go use the bathroom," I said.

"Thanks for the update," Darren Woods said, and the other guys snickered.

Real nice. I slipped through the crowd, looking for Kerri, or even Lindsey and Janice and their dates, who we were supposed to meet here. When I didn't find any of them, I decided to look for an actual bathroom on this floor. Maybe I could hide out for a few minutes until Josh came back. I found myself in the kitchen, where Grace Ricardo, Hailey Berkowitz, and Kyla Danning were hanging out by the keg. Corey and Elena were sitting at the kitchen table, talking in hushed tones. I didn't want to interrupt a lovers' chat—especially these two lovers—but I didn't have many options. It wasn't as if I had ever actually talked to Grace, Hailey, and Kyla.

"Hey, Haskell," I said.

They both looked up. Corey grinned. Elena might as well have been sucking on a lemon.

"Whaddup, Donny?" he asked.

"Have you seen Kerri or Janice and Lindsey anywhere?" I asked, ignoring the death glare I was getting from his on-again girlfriend.

"I think I saw Kerri go upstairs with Drew Spencer," he said.

"Oh, ew! Really?" I asked.

Corey laughed. "Not like that. They were looking for a bathroom."

"Isn't everyone?" I said under my breath. "Thanks."

I turned and headed back toward the stairs. The couple was still on the floor, but now they were on top of each other. I grimaced and stepped over them. Every last one of the seven doors was closed. Who knew what was going on behind them? Definitely nothing I wanted to walk in on. I was just about to lean against a wall and wait when the couple on the floor started writhing around.

So unsanitary.

Behind me was the now-closed door to Josh's mom's OFF LIMITS! room. I turned and shoved it open. The scene that greeted me was so surreal that for a split second I felt like I was falling.

Kerri and Josh stood in the middle of the red throw rug. His arms were locked around her waist, and she was pushing him away.

"Get off me!" Kerri demanded.

Josh looked up and saw me. In that split second his defenses were down, and Kerri slapped him across the face, hard enough that the people on the floor behind me heard it and stopped what they were doing. For a moment we all just stood there, staring at each other.

"Quinn, I'm sorry," Kerri said.

I was already trembling. "What the hell is going on?"

"He followed me in here," Kerri said. She was shaking, too. I found this to be the most disturbing thing of all. Kerri never got shaken. "He's . . . he's been coming on to me all summer."

"Josh?" I said. He rolled his eyes and turned away from us both.

I felt as if the entire room was tilting in front of me. And suddenly it all hit me. Josh getting all psyched about acting opposite Kerri in the Spirit Show. Josh inviting me and *Kerri* to swim. Josh asking me if Kerri hated him. Josh inviting both of us to the party. He had liked Kerri all along.

"Why didn't you tell me?" I asked her.

"Because I knew you'd flip out," she said. "Besides, it's

not like I liked him back. I just figured he'd go away. But you don't go away, do you?" she asked Josh.

"Gimme a break," Josh said, making a condescending face. "Don't get all dramatic on me."

Suddenly I felt my hands curl into fists. I walked up to Josh and somehow looked him in the eye. "I just have one question. If you liked Kerri all along, then what was all that crap about me and Owen? Why did you . . . why did you kiss me?"

I was so proud that my voice didn't waver when I asked this. Everything was crumbling around me, but I sounded totally calm.

"Please," Josh said with a short laugh. "You totally wanted it."

So he wasn't just a slut. He was an asshole as well. I wanted to punch him. I wanted to grab him and throw him out the window. I wanted to tear his hair out. He was such a jerk and he was just standing there, all cocky, like he'd done nothing wrong.

And then the strangest thing happened. A toilet flushed.

We all turned to see Drew Spencer walking out of Josh's mother's state-of-the-art bathroom.

"Whaddup?" he asked, taking in the scene.

"Oh, Josh just tried to kiss me," Kerri said pointedly. She had a mischievous glint in her eye. What was she doing?

"What? This guy?" Drew said as if Josh were some social leper. He stepped up to Josh, crossed his arms over his chest, and lifted his chin. "You make it a habit of attacking other people's dates while they're in the next room?"

Josh smirked. "You gotta be kidding me."

I saw something move out of the corner of my eye and realized the couple from the floor had now walked into the room. A few other people were crowded around outside, watching the show.

"Or how about using girls to get to their best friends?" Kerri asked.

"Or bashing other guys just to pump up your own ego?" I asked.

"Oh, well, he needs that," Kerri told me matter-of-factly. "I hear he's not packing much below the belt, if you know what I mean."

Everyone behind us laughed. I could feel the crowd growing.

Josh's face flushed. "You'd better get out of my face, Spencer," he said to Drew.

"Really?" Drew said, stepping even closer. A flicker of fear passed over Josh's face, and for the first time I noticed that Drew really did have quite a set of shoulders on him. "What are you going to do about it? Cuz I think I'd like to stay here and let them insult you a little bit more," he said, tilting his head toward me and Kerri.

"Oh, I don't know," I said, looking at Kerri and shrugging. "No manners, no life, no standards—"

"No manhood," she reminded me.

Everyone cracked up laughing.

"Right! Right. I forgot about that," I said. "I think our

job is done here. Drew?"

He raised his eyebrows at us.

"Down, boy," Kerri said.

Drew cracked a smile. "I do love a strong woman," he said, shaking his head.

I walked past them, grabbed our clothes out of the closet, then dragged Drew away from Josh with my free hand.

"What can I say? They want me!" Drew said, throwing his hands up as we made our exit.

The crowd parted to let us through, and I shot one last glance at Josh. He leaned back against a wall and bent forward slightly, squeezing his brow with his thumb and forefinger. He really had been scared.

Everyone around us was laughing and rolling their eyes. Suddenly I realized I was done. My first crush was officially over. For the life of me I couldn't remember what I had ever seen in Josh Marx.

That night at the dance I stood next to the punch bowl and took it all in. The gym looked incredible with the autumn-themed decorations and the thousands of white twinkle lights. Corey and I really had done an amazing job, and he, for one, was clearly enjoying every minute of it. He and Elena had been dancing in the center of the floor all night long, barely letting go of each other for a second at a time. Meanwhile, Max had arrived with Grace Ricardo, and every time she moved, he followed her. It was kind of like watching a girl and her dog.

182

I kept seeing both guys in the crowd, wondering what would have happened if I had chosen one of them. Would I be here with a date right now, or would everything have self-imploded just as it had with Owen?

*Yeah, like that really self-imploded,* I thought, picking up the ladle and pouring myself a cup of punch. *That one was all your own fault.*

I had let myself get sucked in by Josh Marx and broken the heart of a perfectly good guy. What was *wrong* with me? Why was I so clueless?

Well, at least I'd learned my lesson. I was never going to let Josh Marx affect me again. And the next time I had a shot with a good guy I was going to give it every chance possible.

"Uh, Quinn?"

I glanced away from the dance floor to find Owen standing on the other side of the table. I felt as if the ground had just dropped out from under me. We hadn't spoken one word to each other since the evil lunchtime breakup. He wore a suit that was slightly too big and a tie that was slightly too short, but he still looked adorable. His face was already blotchy, and he was holding a small square of paper in both hands.

"Hey, Owen," I said.

"I . . . I wanted to give this to you," he said. "It's a little late, but I figured if I didn't do it now, I was never going to do it."

He held out the paper, and I took it, confused. It was folded up tightly, one of the ends stuck under a triangular flap. The edges were worn, as if it had been toyed with a lot. It took me a second to get it open, but when I finally did, my mouth went dry. It said, in juvenile, guy handwriting:

Dear Quinn,
I think you're the coolest. Would you ever want to be my girlfriend?
Sincerely,
Owen Meyer

Oh. My. God. The girl he liked in eighth grade. The one he wrote a note to but never had the guts to give to her. It was me. And he had saved the note all this time. I felt like bursting into tears.

"Owen—"

"Do you want to dance?" he asked. He looked half-hopeful, half-petrified. I knew the feeling.

I wanted to apologize. I wanted to throw myself at his mercy. I wanted to tell him I was the biggest, dumbest, most gullible chick on the planet. But dancing seemed like a much simpler prospect.

"Definitely," I said.

He grinned his heart-stopping grin, and together we walked to the dance floor. I had no idea where this was going, but for now I didn't care. All I had wanted for the past five years was to be with Josh Marx, and apparently all Owen had wanted in that time was to be with me. Me. Quinn "Tomboy" Donohue.

I was flattered, awed, humbled, and totally touched. As Owen took me into his arms on the dance floor, all I knew was that I was going to give him a hell of a lot more respect than *my* unrequited crush had given me.

And maybe, if he still wanted it, I'd also give him a third shot at that kiss.

The End

(or not . . . turn the page!)

# The Choice Redux

$Feel$ like maybe I'm settling here? Wondering if my true love is still out there? If so, go back to page 85 and try again.

# You Chose Corey

## eight

I had to make a move, and I had to do it fast. Something about Max's body language told me that he was about to pounce, and Owen was staring me down like a cartoon dog would look at a cartoon steak. I turned around and looked helplessly at Corey. As if he could do anything to help me. He had no idea what was going on!

Max made a sudden movement, and that was all I needed. Panic ensued.

"So, Corey! I would *love* to go to that movie with you!" I said loudly enough to bring down the school.

Everyone froze. Corey shot me a bemused smile. "Great!" he shouted back. "Is this how we're talking now? Cuz I like it!"

I laughed and, because Owen and Max were still

hovering, leaned over to kiss him on the cheek. Corey flushed. I couldn't believe this was me. But I guess that's what happens when a girl gets herself trapped. The key to survival in moments like this was, in my case, total personality reversal.

And it worked. Sort of. Owen turned around and walked quickly out of the auditorium without a word. I felt sick to my stomach with guilt—one of the negatives of dating three guys at the same time. I hoped he was okay and I knew that I would have to talk to him later.

"Uh . . . Quinn?"

And then there was Max. I glanced at him over my shoulder and he was standing there uncertainly, one hand in his pocket, looking like I'd just run over his dog. "What's going on?" he asked.

Okay. I guess I had to deal with this now. I looked at Corey, and somehow he knew that I needed some alone time with Max.

"I'll meet you out in the lobby," he said.

"Thanks."

I could see a little muscle in Max's jaw working as he watched Corey go. He was definitely not happy.

*Okay, just do this fast,* I told myself. *Quick and painless.*

"Listen, Max, I just don't think it's going to work out," I said. And, because he looked confused, I added, "With us."

"Why not?" he asked. It was almost a whine.

Right. Why not? Even as I stood there, part of me still wanted him to kiss me. I still wanted a chance to feel that total exhilaration and suspension of all logic I experienced when he touched me. But sex and attraction were not the only factors at work here. I had to remember that.

"It's just . . . you're really sweet, but it's all a little . . . much," I said.

For a second I thought he was going to make me go into detail—something I *really* didn't want to do—but then he tipped his head back, looked at the ceiling, and groaned.

"Why do girls always say this to me?" he asked.

I pressed my lips together to keep from smiling. Apparently I wasn't the first to feel the claustrophobia Max could inspire.

"I'm really sorry," I said.

He blew out a sigh and shook his head. "It's fine. I hope you and Corey are very happy together," he added with a touch of sarcasm. I guess he needed to get in some kind of dig, which was understandable. As he turned and walked out, I felt as if the room had suddenly expanded. Relief! The hard part was over.

Well, unless you counted the fact that now I was supposedly dating Corey Haskell. Freaky.

I grinned in giddy anticipation and walked out of the auditorium. True to his word, Corey was waiting. We shared a private smile. I don't think either one of us could believe we were actually going to try this.

"Everything cool?" he asked, glancing at the lobby door through which Max had just disappeared.

"Yeah." *Please don't ask me to explain. Please don't ask me to explain. Please don't ask me to—*

"I was going to go to the skate park for an hour or so.

Wanna come?" he asked.

I should have known. Corey was far too self-assured to be thrown by one conversation with another guy. Plus, who knew how much he cared at this point? Maybe Max didn't even register with him.

"Sure," I replied.

Then he reached out, took my free hand, and laced his fingers through mine. Okay, maybe he cared a little.

"This okay?" he asked.

I laughed. "Yeah. Weird but okay."

"Wanna talk weird? I think I had a sex dream about you last night," Corey said.

I blanched. Holy crap.

"Too much information?" Corey asked, somewhere between mortified and amused.

"Maybe."

"Sorry. I'm gonna have to get used to filtering around you now, I guess," he said. "Also weird."

"There's a lot of weirdness here, huh?" I asked, hoping it wasn't enough to kill it. I liked holding his hand. A lot.

"We'll figure it out," Corey said confidently.

"Right. Yeah," I replied. Then we just sort of looked at each other, smiling curiously. We were really doing this. Friends one day, more-than-friends the next.

"Maybe we should just go skate," Corey said finally.

"Yeah," I said, relieved. "Let's."


"Whoo! That was *sick*!" Corey cheered as I popped up next to him on the big ramp at the park. I grinned from ear to ear, having just executed a one-handed-stand, a trick I had only ever managed one other time in my life. I was having a hell of a day on my board. I think it was all the Corey-released endorphins.

"I know," I said, catching my breath.

Corey grabbed me and kissed me, and, if possible, my grin widened.

"Sorry. Was that weird?" Corey said.

"No," I said, my heart pounding as I looked at him. "Do it again."

Corey blinked, flashed a smile that nearly made me fall off the ramp, then placed both his sweaty hands on either side of my face and kissed me, slowly, softly, perfectly. I dropped my board, and it went skittering down into the bowl. Good Lord. Why hadn't we been doing this all along?

"Ew! I don't need to see that!" one of the middle school-ers shouted at us. Corey pulled back and laughed.

"Dude, she's not even a girl," another one of the little twits called.

A total sock to the gut. I mean, shout out my biggest insecurity right in front of my new boyfriend, why don't you? Quinn Donohue, just one of the guys.

Corey shot him a glare that could have burned a hole right through him. "You're gonna want to get out of here now, little man," he said.

And the kids, valuing their lives, skated off as fast as their sub-par skills allowed.

"Don't listen to them," Corey told me. "They won't know anything for another three years at least."

Then he kissed me again and I forgot all about the insult. If I was girl enough for Corey Haskell, former boy-toy of Elena Marlowe, then I was girl enough for anyone. And if kissing was going to be a new bonus to hanging at the skate park, I was going to be spending even more time here than usual. Friends first was clearly the way to go.

"You are never going to *believe* what I just heard," Kerri said when I answered my cell that night.

"What?" I asked, getting up from the couch.

I was watching *Jeopardy!* with my family—a little Donohue obsession—and we had an unstated rule that when the phone rang, you took it out of the living room.

"Remember when we saw Corey and Elena talking this morning?" she said.

My stomach squeezed into a tight little ball. I sat on the edge of a chair at the dining room table on high alert. I'd already had a brief, heart-wrenching IM with Owen tonight, explaining about Corey. Now what was I in for?

"Madagascar!" my mother shouted in the background.

"No! It's Mesopotamia," my father corrected.

"Yeah," I said to Kerri.

"Well, it turns out she *broke up* with Logan Arnott last night, and then this morning she asked Corey to go to some horror movie with her or something," Kerri announced, incredulous.

I felt like I was going to throw up. Elena had asked Corey to the revival before Corey had asked me? This was bad. This was very bad. And maybe a little insulting, too.

Couldn't the boy come up with his own ideas for dates? Did he have to steal them from his ex-girlfriend?

"Electrons!" my brother called out. "Electrons, you moron!"

"Very good, Jack," my mother said proudly.

"Quinn?"

"I'm here," I croaked.

My heart was pounding so fast and shallow, I didn't think it could sustain a person of my size for very long. I got up and walked around, taking deep breaths and trying to chill while my family continued to shout out their answers. It was hard to believe I was having this kind of reaction. Corey and I had just decided to go out. Did this really mean that much to me that quickly?

*Yes,* a little voice in my mind responded. And I knew in that moment that if Corey went back to Elena now I would be crushed. He was mine now. Or, at least, I wanted him to be.

"Jane Austen!" my mom cried.

"No! Charlotte Brontë!" my dad said.

"You guys. It was Henry James," Jack told them facetiously. I rolled my eyes.

"Well, anyway, apparently Corey told her he knew all about the horror movie thing, thank you very much, and he was already planning on asking you," Kerri said. "He told her no."

Instantly my heart swelled. "He did? He said he was already going to ask me?" That was *so* much better.

"Yeah, and Elena, like, flipped out," Kerri said. "Girl's a

total whack job. I don't know why Corey ever went out with her."

"Because he was totally in love with her," I said.

I ran my hand back and forth along the smooth wood of one of the dining room chairs and sighed. One day and already my relationship with Corey was beyond complicated. I guess that's what you get for dating one half of the former couple of the century.

"What if he still is?" I asked, holding my breath.

"He's not," Kerri said firmly. "He told her he wanted to be with you. What kind of guy says that to the girl he's still in love with?"

"I don't know, the kind who doesn't *know* what he wants? The kind who wants to get back at her? The kind who likes to play games?" I said.

"Whoa. Cynical are we?" Kerri said. "Do you really think Corey is any of those guys? If you do, you shouldn't be dating him."

My shoulders slumped. "No. I don't," I admitted. "But what if I'm wrong?"

"Well, then, you have to find out," Kerri said. "Talk to him. Who knows? Maybe he'll be straight with you."

I snorted.

"What? I've heard it's happened before," Kerri argued. "Last year, some guy in—what was it, Montana? Yeah. Some guy in Montana was actually straight with his girlfriend. It was on the news."

I cracked up, and Kerri laughed as well. What would I do without her?

"Katharine Hepburn!" my mother shouted.

"*Audrey* Hepburn," my father corrected.

"Do you people not know anything?" my brother said.

I had to get back there before a smack-down ensued. Feeling much better, I hung up with Kerri and rejoined my family, ready to think about something other than Corey for a while. At least until *Jeopardy!* was over.

I found Corey in the hallway the next morning before homeroom. He was trying to shove his skateboard into his overpacked locker. Crushed papers, gym clothes, books, and lunch bags all tried to make their escape to the floor. For a politician and straight-A student, he was surprisingly disorganized. How had he accumulated so much stuff when the year had just started? A mystery that I would probably unravel if I kept dating him. Of course, we would know in a few seconds whether that was going to happen or not.

"Donny!" Corey said, pushing everything inside and quickly slamming the locker door before it could fall out again. "How's it going?"

"Okay," I said, clutching a couple of books against my stomach. He didn't kiss me in greeting. Should I expect him to, or was that too PDA for a couple who had been "just friends" a few days ago? Of course, there had been plenty of PDAs at the skate park yesterday. Had something changed since then?

I was really no good at this.

"Oh," he said. "Doesn't look okay."

Man, he's good with body language.

197

"Listen, I heard about your argument with Elena yesterday—"

"I'm not surprised," he said. "Our grapevine's working more like the Internet lately."

He didn't seem remotely embarrassed. Good sign or bad?

"Well, I just wanted to tell you that if you wanted to go to the movie with her, I would totally understand," I said in a rush. "I mean, I won't be mad."

And then I loathed myself. What was I, some kind of doormat? No. A doormat just laid there. I was actively getting out of the way. But what was I supposed to do? Wait around to get trampled on by Elena's high heels when Corey welcomed her back with open arms?

"Sorry?" Corey said, a little wrinkle forming over his nose.

"I mean, it's Elena," I said, like it was that obvious. "Come on. You can't tell me you don't want to go with her."

"Yes. I can," Corey said firmly. "Look, I asked *you* to go to the movie, not Elena," he added. "It's not like I'm gonna drop at her feet just because she suddenly decided to be jealous. One night she sees us out together, and then all of a sudden she wants me back? Please."

I smirked. So he knew exactly what was going on. Why had I thought he would be snowed by her? Corey was one of the smartest guys I knew.

"Okay," I said. "I just wanted to check."

"We good?" Corey asked, studying my eyes.

"We're good," I said, relieved.

"Good."

Then he smiled, leaned in, and planted a quick but firm kiss on my lips. Right there. In the middle of the crowded hallway.

My heart felt like it was being tickled by a thousand little feathers. Was it actually possible that Corey liked me more than Elena Marlowe?

Strange. But also very, *very* cool.

# nine

"Wait, wait, wait. I bet she goes up to the attic," Corey whispered into my ear, sending tingles all the way down my spine. "How much you wanna bet she goes up to the attic?"

"No! She seems like a smart girl. She knows there's a psychotic killer on the loose. Why would she go to the attic?" I replied with mock cluelessness.

Corey laughed. "So naïve, Donny," he joked. "You are just so very naïve."

I grabbed a handful of popcorn and munched on it contentedly, resting a foot on the empty seat in front of me. Corey and I had nabbed prime back-row seats for the horror revival and pretty much bought out the snack bar. For the last hour we had tried out various combinations— Sno Caps and gummy bears (not bad), popcorn with peanut M&Ms (awesome), nacho cheese on pretzel (*soooo* good)—all the while mocking the movie, which was far more entertaining than just sitting there and watching it. And the best part was, no one around us seemed to mind. They were all doing the same thing.

"Here it is," Corey said, sitting up straight and dumping half his popcorn onto the floor. "She can either go outside or upstairs. Which do you think it'll be?"

"Upstairs! Upstairs! Upstairs!" a few guys down front chanted loudly.

As soon as the damsel on the screen turned for the stairs, the whole theater groaned and clapped and laughed. Corey stood up and raised his arms over his head.

"Aw, yeah, baby! Here we go! Told you!" he said as he sat down again.

I threw some popcorn into his face in response. Corey picked a piece off his sweater, shrugged, and popped it into his mouth. I laughed and hunkered down to watch the girl get slashed so I could critique the fake blood. I couldn't remember the last time a movie had been this much fun.

After the final fake-you-out scare (which no one was faked-out by) Corey and I boarded home, talking over the finer cinematic moments. When we got there, we paused on the sidewalk, and I popped up my board.

"I gotta say, movies with you are way more fun than movies with Elena," he said.

I felt the rush of the compliment and the sting of her name all at once. "Why?" I asked.

"She *hated* when I talked during movies," he said. "I

swear she would have lasted about five minutes tonight before flipping into drama mode and storming out."

I smiled. "I'm not much for drama."

"I know," Corey said, suddenly growing serious.

He took a step closer to me, placed his hand on the back of my neck, and pulled me in for a kiss. My heart swooped as our lips met and before I knew it we were kissing and kissing and kissing, our whole bodies pressed together. My very skin pulsated and I swear if we had been anywhere private instead of standing in front of my house, I would have let him do things to me I never even thought of in the closet with Max.

Who knew I could be so attracted to Corey Haskell? I should have kissed him ages ago.

"Hey! Get a room!"

We sprang apart and I glared up at my brother, hanging out the window of his bedroom.

"You're such an asshole, Jack!" I shouted.

He cackled and slammed the window shut.

Corey took my hands and laced his fingers through mine. "Maybe we *should* get a room."

The world spun. "What?" I croaked.

Corey's eyes went wide. "No! I didn't mean *get a room* as in get a room at a motel or something and—Oh, God."

"What?" It was the only word I could think of.

Corey laughed and shook his head. "Nice one, Haskell. I just meant it would be nice to be alone. With you. Sometime. That's all."

I took a deep breath. A million thoughts crowded my

mind. I wanted to be alone with Corey, too. But what did that mean, exactly? I mean, he'd been with Elena "Sexpot" Marlowe for two years. One could only imagine what the two of them had done in *their* alone time. Not that one wanted to. But sometimes, like now, one couldn't exactly stop oneself.

Images flooded my mind. Elena changing for gym. Her lacy bra, her uncontrollable breasts, her thong. Her *thong*. The girl wore a thong to *gym*.

Oh, God. Next to Elena I was the biggest virgin on the planet. Wait. I *was* the biggest virgin on the planet.

"Quinn? Are you gonna say something? Cuz the way your mouth is hanging open right now is freaking me out," Corey said.

I snapped my mouth closed and tried to clear my brain. "I have to get inside."

"Did I say something wrong?" Corey asked.

"No. It's fine. I'm fine," I said. "I just . . . have to pee."

It was the first thing that came to mind. Yes, I am a loser.

"Oh. Okay, then," Corey said. "I guess I'll see you tomorrow."

"Yeah. See ya."

He kissed me quickly, and then I ran into the house, chased by all my insecurities.

The next evening I was onstage in the auditorium, blocking the routine for "Beauty School Dropout" with Kerri, Josh, and Maura Black, dancer extraordinaire. Josh Marx was right next to me, practically breathing down my neck, and all I could think about was Corey. Corey, Corey, Corey.

My, how things had changed.

The boy in question was on the other side of the stage helping Lindsey with one of the silver backdrop panels, but I could feel him looking at me. Neither one of us had mentioned yesterday's "get a room" uncomfortableness, and I truly hoped he wasn't going to bring it up after rehearsal. I was so angry at Jack for starting the whole thing. I was *just* beginning to get over my Elena insecurity, and now it had taken over again.

Corey wanted to be alone with me. *Alone* alone. What if I couldn't measure up? What if Corey realized he'd made a huge mistake and went back to her? Maybe a guy-free existence was the way to go. This was far too stressful.

"Quinn, what do you think of this?" Maura asked me.

I snapped back to the present and watched her as she sashayed across the stage. Corey caught my eye from behind Maura and smiled. My heart turned to goo. I smiled back. Okay, having a guy around had its perks.

"Good. I like it," I told Maura. I know nothing about dancing, so I figured I'd just let her do whatever she wanted.

"This is going to kick ass," Kerri said.

"Tell me about it," I replied, glancing around the bustling auditorium.

About twenty-five or thirty seniors had shown up for the first rehearsal, including a bunch of jocks Josh had recruited. We had to work at night after everyone's athletic practices were over. Aside from us, our advisor Ms. Henderson, and a couple of janitors, the school was deserted. So we *all* had a collective heart attack when the door to the auditorium opened loudly and Elena Marlowe strode in.

Everyone stared in surprise, but to me it *felt* like everyone was staring in awe. Elena was the natural center of attention in any room and too beautiful for anyone to look away from. How did she always look that perfect?

"What's she doing here?" Kerri asked.

"I have no idea."

Elena dropped her bag onto a chair, climbed the steps to the stage, and walked right over to Corey and Lindsey. Corey's face lit up when he saw her, and Lindsey shot me a concerned look. I felt like my insides had been hollowed out. Or maybe his excitement was just a figment of my paranoia. Maybe he was just surprised, too.

"Hey. What're you doing here?" Corey asked.

Everyone tried to pretend they weren't paying attention. Badly.

"I'm here to rehearse," she replied. "Where do you want me?"

"Rehearse," Corey repeated flatly.

"Yeah! I'm the angel, right?" she said with wide-eyed innocence.

My heart thumped with foreboding. Corey shot me a look from across the stage. Slowly Lindsey walked over to join me and Corey, probably sensing there was an argument coming and I might need backup.

"Uh . . . actually, after you left the meeting the other day, Quinn recast the role," Corey said.

*Thanks for putting it all on me,* I thought.

Now it was Elena's turn to shoot me a look. "Oh, please. With who?" she asked Corey.

"With me," Kerri said. She crossed her arms over her chest and squared off with Elena from all the way across the stage.

"This should be good," Josh said under his breath.

"Gimme a break. You?" Elena said, walking casually toward Kerri. "I thought you guys wanted to win this year," she said, addressing the group.

"You did not just say that," Kerri replied, advancing on her.

"Cat fight!" Josh cried gleefully.

No one was trying to pretend they weren't paying attention anymore. I looked around for Ms. Henderson, but she was nowhere to be seen. Probably outside somewhere sneaking a smoke.

"All right. All right. We have a little issue here," Corey said, raising his arms and getting between my best friend and his ex. "No need to overreact."

"Look, no one ever told me the role wasn't mine," Elena said to Corey. "It's not fair. I should still have the part."

Was it just me or did she sound like a petulant five-year-old? I willed Corey to bounce her, but instead he looked helpless.

"She does have a point," he said to me. "When last she left us she was still the angel."

Elena smiled triumphantly. I wanted to drop-kick her right off the stage. Was he really taking her side? Right here in front of all these people?

"Quinn!" Kerri said through her teeth.

"Say something," Lindsey whispered.

Now normally I probably would have heard Elena out and tried to find a compromise, but this wasn't a normal situation. I was jealous and I was irritated and I wanted her gone. Besides, I had a very strong feeling that what I was about to say was right.

"When last she left us she also quit," I said, my skin burning.

"You go, girl," Lindsey said under her breath.

"What?" Elena blurted.

"You said, and I quote, 'If that's what you want to do, I quit,'" I told her, surprised at my own courage. "You quit, and the role was recast. If you want to work backstage, that's fine, but Kerri is playing the guardian angel."

Elena's jaw dropped, and a high-pitched sound came out of her mouth. She turned to Corey with one hand on her hip and glared at him, waiting for him to come to her defense. Corey eyed me over her shoulder.

*Please don't*, I begged silently. *Please don't take her side.*

Corey raised his hands and shrugged. "Girl has a point," he told Elena.

*Thank you!*

"Yes!" Lindsey said, forgetting to whisper this time. She flushed pink and turned away, hiding her face behind her hair. It was all I could do to keep from laughing.

"I don't believe you," Elena snapped at him. Then she whirled around and glared at me, her eyes on fire. "Bet you're really proud of yourself right now."

Actually I was.

"See ya!" Kerri said.

And with that Elena stomped over to the stage stairs. It might have been a more dramatic exit if it hadn't taken so long. She had to get down the steps, grab her bag, and storm all the way up the aisle. By the time the door slammed behind her, half the workers were back to their tasks, talking and laughing.

"Nice one," Kerri said, touching her hand to mine in hidden celebration. Lindsey quickly did the same. But my triumph was short-lived.

"Uh, I think maybe I should go make sure she's okay," Corey said sheepishly. "I'll be right back."

"Oh. Okay," I said. *What? WHAT!?*

He shot me an apologetic look but took off after his ex anyway. What had I gotten myself into here?

If he cared enough to go after her, even when she was clearly wrong, could he really be over her? I'd had three perfectly good guys, and I picked Corey. Now I wasn't at all sure that he was going to pick me.

"I talked to Mrs. Norton, and she said she can round up a bunch of white graduation gowns from last year," Corey said as we walked down the crowded hallway before first period. "We can use those for the angels."

"Perfect!" I said, checking that off my list. I was in the homecoming zone. I was not thinking about Elena. Not at all. "I'm getting aluminum foil tonight so we can make the wings and the curler things."

"Curler things?" Corey asked.

"Yeah, for the guys to wear on their heads," I reminded him.

"Right," he said. "What about Josh's outfit?"

"Got it covered," I told him. "Janice's mother has a fifties Halloween costume she's lending us. She's gonna let out the waist."

"Nice! We are such a killer team," Corey said.

"I know," I replied, practically glowing.

Up ahead, Elena and a couple of her friends rounded the corner and walked in our direction. Amazing. It didn't matter how hard I tried not to think about her. She was everywhere. My body heat soared as I wondered if she was going to say something or if Corey was going to say something or if everything was suddenly going to come crashing down on me. Instead, Corey reached out and took my free hand in his. My heart leapt.

See? He was so mine.

I was smiling as Elena slid by. She tried to stare straight ahead and ignore us, but I saw her eyes dart to our clasped hands, and I swear she blanched a little bit. Ha! Then I looked at Corey, and my heart dropped. He was smirking. Triumphantly.

Oh, no way.

Had he taken my hand solely to win that reaction from

Elena? Was he just using me to get back at her? Was that what this was all about? He wasn't over her. I knew it!

I was about to pull my hand away when Josh stepped out of a classroom and almost slammed right into us.

"Hey," he said.

I saw him notice our hands as well. He did a double take. I can't say I'm proud, but instead of pulling away, I tightened my grip. Oh, crap. Was *I* not over *Josh?*

"I got the pink wig," Josh told us, recovering from whatever surprise he had just experienced. "We're good to go."

"Cool," Corey said. "This is gonna kick ass."

"You know it," Josh said.

As soon as Josh was gone, Corey picked up our entwined hands and kissed the back of mine, smiling into my eyes. Instantly I felt guilty for enjoying Josh's surprise.

Who knew dating was this complicated?

When I arrived at the skate park that night, Corey was already out on the ramps. I bought a couple of sodas from the machine and brought them over. When he saw me dropping my stuff onto one of the benches, he skated right over.

"Hey!" he said, planting a welcoming kiss on my lips.

I grinned and flushed. I wasn't totally used to kisses-in-greeting yet. He was winded and sweating, and his lips tasted salty. "Hi," I replied. "Soda?"

"Oh! Just what I need," he said. He popped open the tab and downed half the contents in one gulp. "You're such a good little girlfriend," he teased.

"Ha-ha," I replied automatically. Then I sat down on the bench and looked up at him, my pulse suddenly racing. "Is that what I am? Your girlfriend?"

I was thinking about Elena. I was wondering if *he* was thinking about Elena. I was wondering if he could possibly think of anyone other than Elena as his girlfriend.

Corey blinked. "Aren't you?"

"I . . . I guess I—"

Was this the way this conversation was supposed to happen? Backward and confused, with me wondering about his ex? Out in the distance the sun sank toward the horizon, and birds chirped in the trees all around us. It felt like there was supposed to be something a lot more romantic going on.

"Actually, before you answer that question, let me ask you this one," Corey said, sitting next to me.

He set down his soda and took off his helmet. He slid out his backpack from under the bench and pulled out a towel to mop his face. Through all of this I felt like I was about to keel over with anticipation. What was the question? What was the *question*?

Finally he looked me in the eye and let out a breath. "Will you go to the homecoming dance with me?"

I smiled, feeling tingly all over. Really. All over. "Definitely," I said.

"Good," Corey replied, his grin matching mine. "And will you also be my girlfriend?"

There was a moment of silence in which I tried not to, but—I couldn't help it—I started laughing.

"What?" Corey asked.

"I'm sorry, it just . . . it sounded so funny the way you said that," I said between gasps. "Like, I don't know, some *Seventh Heaven* episode or something."

"Wow. Nice. Give a guy a break!" Corey complained, but he was smiling. "Or at least give him an answer."

"Yes," I said, nodding and trying to regain control. "Yes, Corey, I will be your girlfriend."

He looked at me again, and we *both* burst out laughing. In its own very unique and messed-up way, the moment was romantic.

When he kissed me, I didn't even wonder if he was thinking about Elena. Well, at least I didn't wonder about it for more than five seconds.

A definite improvement.

# ten

Friday afternoon I was in the kitchen with my mom, innocently peeling potatoes for dinner, when my cell phone rang. I saw on the caller ID that it was Corey, and I grabbed it. Girly giddiness everywhere.

"Hey."

"Hey. Guess what?" he said.

"Bill Clinton finally returned one of your many e-mails?" I joked.

"Better. My parents are going to a wedding tomorrow night, and they're staying over."

My stomach officially left my body. I glanced at my mom, who hummed along with the radio while she started to chop. I turned away from her.

"And?" I said. Even though I knew where this was going.

"Wanna come over? Rent a movie . . . ?"

*Have sex?* I finished silently.

Oh, God. Oh, God, oh, God, oh, God. Had I really gotten this far this fast? And why did I feel so psychotically exhilarated and so ready to heave at the same time?

"Hang on a sec," I told him. I covered the phone and clenched my entire body. "Mom? Can I hang out at Corey's tomorrow night?"

*Say no. No. Say yes. Say no. No. Wait. I don't—Screw it.*

"Sure, honey." She looked at me as if she was wondering why I was even asking. That was what happened when you never did anything to make your parents mistrust you.

There was nothing I could do but get back on the phone and say, without breathing, "Okay. I'm there."

"I cannot believe that Quinn Donohue just walked through the doors of Victoria's Secret," Kerri said. "Can I get a witness?"

"Shhhh!" I said, grabbing her raised hand and turning red, then green. A woman in a tight, short little suit hustled our way, weaving around racks of masochistic underwear.

"Can I help you girls with something?"

"No, thanks. We're fine," I said, yanking Kerri toward the back of the store.

"My name is Rebecca if you need anything!" the worker bee called after us.

"Thank you, Rebecca!" Kerri called back. She was loving every minute of this.

I ducked into a corner behind a sale rack and put my

214

face into my hands. "Do you *have* to humiliate me?" I asked.

I felt as if every single shopper in the store was staring at me. And why not? In my ripped jeans and oversized T-shirt, I didn't exactly blend. I looked like I should be buying my underwear at Old Navy. Which was where most of it came from.

"I'm sorry," Kerri said. "I'm sorry. I'll stop."

"I mean, like it isn't bad enough that I might be having *sex* tonight," I hissed. "I'm already nervous enough to puke."

"Okay! Okay!" Kerri said. "I'm here for you, babe. And I'm honored that you asked me to come with you to pick out your first adult underwear. I have to say, I'm very impressed."

"Thanks. I just don't want Corey comparing me to Elena," I said.

Kerri scoffed. "News flash. Corey is going to be comparing you to Elena. He's going to be comparing you to any and all girls he's had the good fortune of seeing in their Skivvies."

If I wasn't hyperventilating before, I was now. "Geez, Ker. You really know how to make me feel better."

"What? It's totally natural," Kerri said. And when I just stared at her, she gave me a fed-up look. "Like you didn't compare your first kiss with Corey to your first kiss with Max."

I blinked. She had me there.

"See? Everyone does it," Kerri said. "But don't worry. Elena has nothing on you."

"How do you figure?" I asked sarcastically.

"Because you are human, whereas she is a demon yanked from the bowels of hell."

Now there was a visual. But it made me laugh.

"Okay," I said, taking a deep breath. "Where do we start?"

Kerri looked around. "Black and lace are always good."

I swallowed a lump that formed in my throat at the very sight of the bras she had honed in on. I couldn't believe I was spending my allowance money on underwear instead of the new iPod I'd been saving up for. But this was for Corey. If he *was* going to compare me to his ex, this was my only shot.

"You ready?" Kerri asked me.

I stood up straight and squared my shoulders like I was going into battle. "Let's do it."

That night I sat on the couch in Corey's living room not watching *Hitch* but wondering when he was going to make his move. My new bra dug into the undersides of my breasts like a knife, and the G-string Kerri had somehow talked me into shifted uncomfortably every time I squirmed. Did people really wear these torture devices every day? How did they concentrate on anything?

I glanced over at Corey uncertainly. Maybe it was my fault that he hadn't jumped me yet. When I got there, he sat down at the end of the couch. I thought about cuddling right into him, but it felt too forced. I'd watched half a dozen movies at his house and I'd never cuddled with him before.

So instead I took the center of the couch. Close enough to hear him breathing but too far away for him to touch me.

Every five seconds I thought about just leaning over and kissing him. Or tearing off my shirt. I mean, if he never got to see this stupid bra, then I would have gone through all that humiliation for no reason. He *had* to see it. When were we going to do this already?

Corey laughed at something in the movie, and I faked a laugh as well. I glanced at him, and he smiled. Then, suddenly, finally, he leaned toward me. This was it. He was going in! I closed my eyes and puckered up and hoped for the best. . . .

But Corey just brushed right by me, picked up the bowl of pretzels on the table, and leaned back.

My body was so hot, I was sure the underwires were melting. I couldn't take it anymore. I picked up the remote and paused the movie.

"When are we going to do this?" I blurted.

Corey paused with a pretzel halfway into his mouth. "Do what?" he asked.

*Just do it,* I heard Kerri say in my mind. *Make a move. Face your fear.*

I sighed, waited for him to chew and swallow, then lunged at him. Corey was obviously taken aback for a split second, but finally he turned onto his back and settled in, kissing me back. Suddenly I found myself lying on top of him, one knee between his legs, one elbow pressed into his armpit. I felt heavy and awkward, and I had no idea what I was doing. How had I ended up on *top?*

217

Corey wasn't doing anything. He was just lying there letting me kiss him, his hands resting motionless on my back. Shouldn't he be going for my bra? Or was I supposed to go for his belt? I couldn't do that, could I?

This was awful. All I could think about was what I was supposed to do next, and I couldn't even concentrate on the kissing. Plus he tasted like fresh pretzel. Finally I pushed myself up so that I was sitting sideways on his legs.

"What's wrong?" Corey asked, propping himself up on his elbows.

I shoved my hair out of my face and tried not to cry. I felt hot, humiliated, and totally stupid.

"Nothing," I said unconvincingly.

Corey looked around the room, confused. "What just happened here?"

"Nothing," I said again. "I just—"

"Quinn, what were you talking about when you said, 'When are we going to do this?'" Corey asked me.

If possible, my cheeks flushed even harder. "Nothing. I was just . . . I thought . . . you know . . . your parents are out . . . you wanted to be alone. . . . "

Corey blinked and his brow creased. He pushed himself up so that I had to slide off his legs. He sat sideways on the couch, facing my profile. I pulled my legs up and hugged them to me, avoiding eye contact at all costs. I would bet a zillion dollars that Elena had never done anything like this. If she wanted to have sex with Corey she probably would have come over here in nothing but a raincoat and heels and taken charge.

"Quinn, did you think I invited you over here just to have sex?" he asked.

"Well, yeah," I half-wailed, sounding like a big baby. I looked at him and he smiled, amused, which did not make me feel better. "You said you wanted to be *alone* with me and everything. I don't know. I figured you wanted to . . . do stuff."

Corey reached over and picked up my hand, which I reluctantly let him do. "Yeah, I wanted to be alone with you. And yeah, 'doing stuff' was on my mind. But I wasn't expecting, you know, *that*," he said.

"So you *don't* want to have sex with me?" I blurted.

"No!" Corey replied. "I mean, yes! Of course. Are you kidding? Do you have any idea how hot you are? Who wouldn't want to have sex with you?"

I grinned. This was much better. "So, why weren't you expecting it?"

Corey clucked his tongue and sighed. "I don't know. It's you. And me. We're still figuring out how to hold hands and not feel like total freaks. So I'm totally fine with taking it slow in the, uh . . . ." He cleared his throat. "Sex. Area."

I think I was in love. Seriously. In that moment I was fairly certain of it.

I turned to completely face him and held his hand for real. "How slow, exactly? Cuz I got this new bra . . . "

Corey's eyes lit up. "*Real*-ly?"

I flushed, smiled, and shrugged. "And it would be a serious waste for you not to see it."

I couldn't believe I was saying this, but that's how

comfortable I felt with him. This was Corey. And I didn't feel scared. Nervous and excited, but not scared. And from the look on his face I knew he was thinking only about me. No one else. And he was *dying* to see what was under my T-shirt. No one else's.

I looked into his eyes.

"We're really going to do this?" he said. "You and me."

"Shut up and kiss me," I said.

And he did. And it was perfect. Everything we did that night was perfect.

# eleven

"Omigod, I'm starving!" I said, speed-walking toward the food court on Sunday afternoon. "Can we get Taco Bell? I'm jonesing for shredded chicken."

"You can have whatever you want," Kerri said, following me with our bags. "I still can't believe I got you to the mall two days in a row."

"Well, a girl needs a homecoming dress," I said happily.

"Okay, who are you, and what have you done with my best friend?" she asked, raising her eyebrows. "Seriously a little frightened over here."

"What?" I said as the concourse opened up into the rotunda of the food court. "I'm just in a good mood."

"No, I think you're in love," Kerri said.

I laughed. I think I almost twirled around, but I

managed to stop myself in time, playing it off like I was avoiding an old lady with a walker.

"You *are!* You're in loo-oo-*ove*!" Kerri sang, teasing me. "Quinn and Corey sitting in a tree! K-I-S-S . . ."

She trailed off before the *I-N-G*, and her face fell. I turned around to figure out what had stunned her into silence and my stomach flipped over. It was Corey. And Elena. Standing in line together at Ranch 1. Talking. Laughing. Together.

I ducked behind a huge potted plant and peeked out. Kerri joined me, peeking out the other side. I watched Corey step to the front of the line and order. Elena looked up at him adoringly, and I felt his hands on my skin. I felt his lips on my lips. I felt his fingers grazing my cheek.

And I felt dirty. Used and dirty and sick.

"Don't panic," Kerri said. "Maybe they're not here together."

But even as she said it, Corey and Elena got their trays. When Corey stepped away from the crowd we could see that he was carrying not only his food but a bunch of bags. The Abercrombie and Fitch might have been his, but the Rampage, the French Connection, and the *Victoria's Secret* certainly were not.

Numb from head to toe, I stepped away from the tree and turned around.

"Where're you going?" Kerri asked.

"I'm not in the mood for tacos anymore."

"You have to talk to him," Kerri whispered as we bumped a volleyball back and forth in gym class the next day.

Around us dozens of other pairs did the same with varying degrees of success. Every once in a while there'd be a "Heads up!" and everyone would hit the deck to avoid a kamikaze ball.

"Actually I think the fact that I screened his calls all night and avoided him all morning proves the exact opposite," I said. I was angry and desperate and I took it out on the volleyball. It went sailing over her head.

Kerri grabbed the ball out of the air. "Wow. That was sarcastic."

"Yeah, well, I learned from the best," I told her, taking the ball back.

"If you won't talk to him, maybe I will," Kerri said as I served the ball to her.

"You will not," I told her.

"Someone's gotta find out what's going on," she said.

"Heads!" someone shouted.

Kerri and I both ducked as a ball zipped past our heads and slammed into the bleachers. My heart took a nosedive when I saw Elena herself jogging over to retrieve it. Kerri stared at me meaningfully. I stared back and shook my head.

"Do it," she said through her teeth.

"Shut up," I said back.

Elena was striding away when Kerri opened her mouth. "Hey, Marlowe."

I was going to kill her. I really was. Death by volleyball.

Elena turned around slowly, holding the ball between her wrist and her hip. "Lawrence," she said. She just glanced at me like I was dirt.

*Corey*

"Don't," I said under my breath.

Kerri ignored me. "Saw you at the mall yesterday," she said.

"Oh, really?" Elena said, taking a couple of steps toward us. "I'm shocked that you didn't say hello."

Kerri smirked. This train ride was completely out of my control. "What were you and Corey doing there together?"

My mouth was completely dry. All I wanted was to get the heck out of there. Elena looked at me and smiled slowly. "If you have something to ask me, why don't you ask me yourself?" she said.

I wanted to punch her. Kerri stepped closer to me, and I took a deep breath.

"Do you want him back?" I asked. My voice croaked, but I managed to look her in the eye.

"Well, since you asked, yeah. I do," Elena said.

Holy crap. Was she kidding me? She was just going to say this right to my face?

"I thought you were back with Logan," I said.

"I am," she replied with a shrug. "But you know what one of the best things about being a girl is? We get to be fickle."

I had never been so disgusted by someone in my life.

"Why am I not surprised that *you* wouldn't know that?" she said, looking my baggy Adidas shorts and Orioles T-shirt up and down. "Here's a tip. You wanna hold on to a guy, stop dressing like one."

She turned and strode off.

"Oh, I am so going to kick her ass," Kerri said.

But I grabbed her arm and held her back. I couldn't let Kerri fight my battles for me. If anyone was going to kick her ass, it was going to be me. But, of course, we all knew that I wouldn't.

Halfway across the gym Elena turned around. "May the best . . . *person* win," she said pointedly.

And then I *really* wanted to tackle her. But the bell rang. And I was saved.


"So, what're you going to do?" Kerri asked that afternoon as we headed into the auditorium for our second-to-last Spirit Show rehearsal.

"I'm going to trust him," I said, trying to sound more confident than I felt.

"Really?"

I paused at the top of the aisle. Down on the stage several people were milling around, but I hadn't spotted Corey yet.

"Why? I shouldn't?" I asked. "I've been thinking about this all day, and I just don't think he would screw me over like that."

"Well, I don't know. He is a good guy, right?" Kerri said. "So maybe you're right. But then again, he *is* human."

I dropped down on the armrest of one of the seats. "So you think he'll go back to her?" My heart hurt.

"Not necessarily," Kerri said.

"You're not helping me here," I whined.

Kerri put her bags down. "Okay, look. I think trusting him is a good idea. You should *not* become all whiny and clingy and start asking him where he is at all times and who he's talked to. No matter how tempting it is."

"Right," I said.

"But that doesn't mean you can't take control of some other factors," Kerri said.

"Like what?" I said.

"Like make sure his focus is on you," Kerri said. "Make plans with him. Pick up the phone when he calls. *Flirt* with the guy. Let him know how much you like him. And, most important, look really hot at homecoming."

I made a face. "Thanks for the tip."

"I'm serious. Beat Elena at her own game," Kerri said, glancing toward the stage. "And now would be a really good time to start."

"Why? What's—"

But then I saw them. Standing near the wings were Elena and Corey, and once again she was all up in his face, tossing her hair and smiling.

"Excuse me," I said, riding a sudden wave of anger. I walked down the aisle and flung my things up onto the stage. "All right, people, it's crunch time!" I shouted. "We have only three days to whip this production into shape, and we have a lot of work to do. Now! Mrs. Norton needs help finishing up the costumes in the home ec room, so anyone who is not in the actual production, get your butts over there and see what you can do."

Most of the set crew snapped to and followed my directions, but Elena just stood there.

"That means you, Marlowe," I said.

She narrowed her eyes at me. "Why am I not surprised?"

"Thanks for doing your part," I told her.

Elena grumbled and stormed off the stage. Corey merely shrugged and walked over to me, planting a kiss right on my lips. Sigh.

"Where you been?" he asked. "I missed you."

I smiled, my heart all aflutter. The best person *was* going to win. "I missed you, too."

# twelve

That night I sat at my desk, staring blankly at my history textbook. I was supposed to be reading chapter five and writing three important "talking points" for class tomorrow. Instead, all I could think about was Elena Marlowe. She was so omnipresent in my mind, you'd think I had a crush on her.

I sighed and shifted my gaze to the floor. Sticking out of my backpack was the black notebook I was using for homecoming. I had some work to do on that as well, and somehow that seemed like an easier task than reading about World War I. I tossed the text on my bed and leaned over to pull out the notebook.

At the top of my list of things to do I had to match up couples for the halftime show at the homecoming game. A local classic car collector always lent us five gorgeous autos for the homecoming court to tool around the field in during halftime. Each pair got its own car and would ride up from the school together and around the track. Then they would step up to the stage together to give their speeches. They would also be announced together at the dance that night. Bottom line, you spent a lot of time with that person over the course of the day. I looked down the list of names.

Logan Arnott
Max Eastwood
Corey Haskell
Joshua Marx
Kyle Stoller
Hailey Berkowitz
Kyla Danning
Elena Marlowe
Grace Ricardo
Sharon Stevens

Now, the simple and logical thing to do would be to pair them up according to alphabetical order and call it a day. But I couldn't do that. In a bitter twist of alphabetical irony, that would mean putting Elena on Corey's arm for the entire day. An entire day in which she would be dressed to the nines. An entire day in which she would have him all to herself, to flirt and remind him of all the ways she was superior to me.

Heart pounding as if I was doing something reprehensible, I quickly drew up a list. Corey with Hailey in the first car. Then Josh with Sharon (there was no rule stating I couldn't put him in with the least desirable, was there?), Kyle with Grace, Max with Kyla (Kyle and Kyla would have been bad), and Logan with Elena in the last car.

Hey, they were a couple, weren't they? Of course they should be put together. And was it my fault if Elena's car was the absolute farthest from Corey's?

Well, yeah, it was. But I was in charge. I could do what I wanted. That's one of the perks of power.

Satisfied, I typed up the list, printed it out, and placed it with all the other things I had to hand in to Ms. Henderson. Finally I had done something proactive. Kerri would be proud.

"We are *so* good," Corey whispered in my ear, sending a shiver all through me.

"Tell me about it," I replied.

We were huddled in the wings as Kerri began to descend the ladder at the center of the stage. The audience had already gone into convulsions when the curtain went up and they'd seen Josh in his fake lashes, pink wig, and poodle skirt. Now they applauded when Kerri started to sing, all but drowning out her first lines.

As Kerri sang, her jumpsuit glittering under the lights, Josh clasped his hands under his chin and fluttered his lashes adoringly up at her. The place went wild.

"Damn!" Corey said.

"I know. They're going to bring the place down."

And then half the football, soccer, baseball, and basketball teams fluttered in wearing their white gowns and curlers, and the entire audience was on its feet. Everyone onstage stayed in character—I have no idea how. I couldn't have stopped grinning to save my life.

I watched Leon Monroe and Darren O'Donovan flitting around on tiptoe and laughed, leaning back into Corey's chest. He wrapped his arms around me from behind and rested his chin on my shoulder.

This was perfection. This moment. This guy. This feeling. Nothing could be better.

"We make a kick-ass team," Corey said into my ear. Then kissed my cheek.

"Yes, we do," I replied. I had no idea where Elena Marlowe was at that moment and for once I didn't even care.

By the time Rasheed Stevenson, the biggest linebacker on the football team, was lowered from the rafters with his wings and his harp, the auditorium exploded. I could see that the first three rows at least were on their feet. There was no way we weren't going to win this thing. These people *loved* us!

At last Kerri sang her final line, and the curtain dropped on Josh staring up into the "sky." The ovation continued even as we all cheered ourselves. People flung themselves into one another's arms, and Corey gave me a quick kiss on the lips.

Then, through the din of the crowd, we both heard a

sudden commotion backstage. Up above, Rasheed dipped perilously, and someone shouted for help. Corey blanched. He ran backstage and grabbed at the rope holding Rasheed aloft. Eight guys from the football team were apparently not enough to get all two-hundred-and-fifty-plus pounds of Rasheed lowered safely. As I watched, they regained control, and Rasheed's face registered relief. The moment his feet hit the floor and we knew he was okay, Josh bounded off the stage and grabbed me up in his arms.

My heart went ballistic. Everyone around us cheered and high-fived and screamed in triumph, and Josh Marx was twirling me around. Josh Marx!

"You rock, Quinn Donohue!" he shouted, replacing me on the ground. "That was the most killer Spirit Show ever! You are the master!"

I laughed. Josh was still wearing his pink wig, and beneath his heavy makeup his face was flushed with pleasure and triumph. This had to be one of the most exhilarating moments of our lives. The juniors and their lame-ass rendition of "Look at Me, I'm Sandra Dee" were going down.

"Listen, I know this is out of nowhere, but I don't have a date for the dance yet," Josh said. "You wanna go with me?"

I felt as if the entire world had just dropped out from underneath me. Josh Marx was asking me out! Josh Marx was asking me to the homecoming dance! How many times in my life had I fantasized about this exact moment? And it was totally perfect. He had picked the exact ideal moment, when everything was coming together and I was sitting on top of the world. I couldn't have imagined it better.

Except . . .

I glanced left and saw Corey celebrating with the football team. Corey. I was already going with Corey.

*But this is Josh! Josh Marx!* a little voice in my head wailed. A voice that sounded a lot like my thirteen-year-old self.

*So what?* I replied.

And suddenly I knew. I watched Corey slapping hands with the guys and laughing, and I knew he was the only one I wanted to go with. Josh Marx was so five years ago. A tremendous calm came over me. A calm I had never felt before in Josh's presence. I was about to do something I never in a million years would have thought I could do.

"Thanks. That's really, um, sweet," I said, looking the crush of my life straight in the eye. "But I already have a date."

# thirteen

After school I went searching for Corey. I just couldn't wait to see him. Something inside of me had shifted, and I felt like a new person—capable of anything. Two weeks ago I never would have been able to say no to Josh Marx, but I had, and it felt good. Turning down a person who had ignored me my whole life was about a hundred times more exhilarating than the fact that he had finally noticed me in the first place. And I was only able to do it because of Corey.

I was over Josh Marx. And all I wanted to do was kiss my boyfriend.

He was waiting for me by my locker. I bounded over as giddily as a golden retriever after a ball.

"Hi!" I said, planting a kiss on his lips.

"Hey," he replied.

He was a little stiff and distracted. It put a lull in my kinetic energy.

"What's up?" I asked.

"I have a student government meeting, so I can't really talk, but I wanted to tell you before you heard it from someone else—"

Oh, God. Oh, God, what?

"I'm riding with Elena at the game tomorrow," he said, swallowing.

"You're what?" I blurted. "No, you're not. I already handed in the list."

"I just went by Ms. Henderson's room and changed it," Corey said.

The hallway was spinning. The whole school was spinning. He had gone behind my back to change my work so he could spend the day tied to his ex-girlfriend's side? I really thought I might faint. Or punch something. The giddiness was gone.

"I'm sorry I went around you, but Elena's fighting with Logan, and she was really upset," Corey explained. "She just doesn't want to be forced to be with him. She'd be miserable."

Unbelievable. She had beaten me at my own game. This girl was *good.*

*And what about me?* I wanted to say. *What about how miserable I am? Right now?*

"You don't mind, right?" Corey said, tucking his chin and looking up at me.

*Yeah, I mind! Say it! Say you mind!*

"It's fine," I said, blowing out a sigh. I was a wuss. A nonconfrontational wuss. "Whatever," I added. My passive-aggressive way of telling him I was *not* happy.

Corey grinned. Apparently he didn't get passive aggression. "Great! I'd better go! See you at the bonfire tonight."

He gave me a quick kiss on the cheek and was gone.

Because Corey was in the homecoming processional, it fell to me to announce the homecoming court at halftime the next day. I wore my cleanest jeans and my red and gold Garden Hills Softball T-shirt to show my school spirit. Standing out there in the center of the football field under that bright blue sky, I realized that this was the weekend I had been waiting for since being named co-chair of the committee last year. But I wasn't excited. I was feeling nothing but dread.

"Go ahead, Ms. Donohue," Ms. Henderson whispered, nodding to me from the side of the temporary stage.

Behind me ten chairs were lined up to welcome the homecoming court, plus one for me to take when I was done. In ten minutes Corey and Elena would be sitting there. Together. Looking like the couple they once were.

"Go!"

I cleared my throat and stepped to the microphone. "Hello, everyone, and welcome to this year's Garden Hills High School homecoming festivities. Go, Wildcats!"

The crowd went wild, and I felt a little thrill of exhilaration. It passed quickly.

236

"My name is Quinn Donohue, co-chair of the home-coming committee." I paused for more applause. "And it is my pleasure to introduce to you, your homecoming court!"

On cue, the first car pulled out onto the track, doing about five miles an hour. Sitting atop the backseat of the convertible were Logan Arnott and Hailey Berkowitz. If Logan was bummed about not being matched up with Elena, he wasn't showing it. Still clad in his football uni-form, but *sans* helmet, he cheered and thrust his fist toward the crowd, shouting and riling them up. Hailey smiled and waved jauntily like a Miss America contestant. I would have killed to see Elena in that car instead of her. Killed.

The other cars rolled out one by one. Josh waved but didn't put on as much of a show as Logan. Max, sporting his soccer jersey, looped an arm around Kyla's shoulder and she flushed. In a suit and a tasteful dress, Kyle and Grace looked like they could have been the next Kennedys, all coiffed and buffed and shiny. And then—I held my breath—came the finale. Corey and Elena.

It was even worse than I'd thought. Elena's dark hair hung in gorgeous tendrils over her bare shoulders. She wore a little yellow sundress that showed off her impres-sive curves, and even from across the field it seemed as if the sun was bouncing off her gorgeous legs. As the crowd roared their approval, Corey grinned and waved. Like Kyle, Corey had worn a suit, and he was so handsome, I could have died. He looked at Elena, and they shared a laugh. A private little this-is-so-cool-and-I'm-so-glad-to-be-sharingit-with-you kind of laugh.

*He's still your boyfriend*, I thought, feeling hollow. *He's still taking you to the dance tonight.*

And then, right there in front of me and the entire school, Elena took his hand in hers. Corey smiled, and he didn't let go.

At approximately the time Corey was supposed to be picking me up for the dance, I was racing down the steepest incline at the skate park. Sweating and forcing back tears of frustration, I imagined Corey and Elena dancing under the disco ball in the gym. I wondered if they would win king and queen and get the spotlight dance. I wondered if they would officially get back together on the spot, solidifying their position as perfect high school sweethearts. They would walk hand-in-hand into the center of the crowd, their crowns glinting (the crowns *I* had bought, by the way), and right there, in front of the entire school, kiss like they'd never kissed before.

*Screw it*, I thought, popping up atop the ramp and grabbing my board. *Screw them both.*

I didn't realize I was attempting a 540 until I was all the way through the 360. My heart dipped as I realized I didn't have nearly enough spin to get all the way around. The board hit the ramp at a sick angle, and I braced myself for the crushing fall. Five seconds later I was on my back staring at the sinking sun, gasping for breath and wondering what else could possibly go wrong.

Then the sun was blocked out, and Corey was staring

238

down at me. "What the hell are you doing here?" he demanded. "I was supposed to pick you up half an hour ago."

I pushed myself up to my elbows as one of the kamikaze middle-schoolers zoomed right past my head. The sight of Corey filled me with fresh anger and new hope all at once. He was wearing his suit with a light green tie and clutching a corsage in a plastic box. So, what was the plan? Take me to the dance as a pity gesture and wait until Monday to break up with me?

I stood up, dusted off my butt, and grabbed my board, which had landed wheels up. "Why don't you just go pick up Elena?"

I dropped the board and jumped on, but Corey grabbed my arm before I could get away. I stumbled off and almost fell into him.

"What?" he asked, his eyes flashing.

Two more boarders blew by us. I had a feeling that if we stayed where we were, we would be in mortal peril. I yanked my arm away from him and, when the coast was clear, led him over to the fence.

"Look, I know you really want to be with her. It's fine," I said, even though tears were stinging the back of my eyes. "Just go."

I wanted him to get out of there before I burst out crying. That was the last humiliation I needed.

Corey blew out a breath through his nose and glared at me. "Screw Elena!" he said, squaring his shoulders.

"What?" I couldn't have been more stunned. Hadn't I

just been thinking almost the same thing?

"I don't want to go to the dance with Elena. In fact, I don't want to go anywhere with Elena," Corey said emphatically.

"Could have fooled me," I said.

"What are you talking about?" he asked.

"I'm talking about last weekend," I blurted. "Last Sunday, to be exact. I saw you guys."

"Saw us?"

"Yes! At the mall! Shopping together?" I said. "Don't try to deny it. I saw you with my own eyes."

Corey tipped his head back. "I was at the mall getting a new tie for homecoming, and I *bumped into* Elena in the food court."

"Please! You were carrying her stuff!" I said.

"Yeah, because she couldn't carry it all *and* her tray," Corey responded. "I was there with my mom, Donny. I dropped Elena's tray off and went to eat with my mother. Didn't you see *that?*"

I felt even more ill than before. "No. I kind of left after I saw you carrying her Victoria's Secret bag."

"Well, why didn't you ask me about it?" Corey asked.

"Because Kerri told me not to," I replied.

"Great. How about we don't listen to Kerri anymore?" Corey suggested.

"Well, I didn't know what was going on!" I said, feeling desperate. "And the night before we had just . . . you know."

Corey smiled. "Yeah, I know. Believe me, I know. I've gone over it about ten billion times in my head, so I know."

"Really?" I said, unable to squelch a grin.

Corey stepped forward and put his hands on my shoulders. "Listen to me, because I don't want to have to say this again, all right? I think about you pretty much twenty-four-seven these days. It's kind of crazy. But it's true. I want to be with *you*. No one else. You."

I had to concentrate in order to swallow. "Really?"

"Yes, really," Corey said with a small smile.

"But . . . but what about today? What about riding in the car with Elena and everything?" I asked.

Corey groaned. "She came to me in tears yesterday and begged me not to make her ride with Logan. What was I supposed to do?" he said. "I'm a gentleman, so I said yes. But it was just another one of her psycho mind games."

"Psycho mind games?" I repeated.

"She's been playing me since the moment we first started dating," Corey said. "I'm the idiot who thought she couldn't do it anymore once we were broken up, but that's all it was."

"How do you know?" I asked. I was genuinely interested in how other girls got away with this type of thing.

Corey looked me in the eye. I could tell he was trying to predict how I was going to react to whatever he was about to say.

"She tried to kiss me," he said. "After the ceremony."

"I don't believe this!" I blurted, throwing up my hands and turning away. "I knew it!"

"But I didn't let her!" Corey told me. "In fact I kind of . . . told her off," he added.

When I looked at him again he was grinning wickedly.

"Really?" I said, scrunching my nose.

"That's, like, your favorite word today," Corey said. "Yes, really. Look, Elena is the furthest thing from my mind, all right? You're the only person I care about."

I opened my mouth, but Corey cut me off.

"And if you say 'really,' I might have to kick your ass."

I laughed. My heart did a little happy dance.

"Quinn, I've been looking forward to this dance for three years," he said, walking toward me. "And as senior class president I could actually get into trouble if I don't show. But if you don't want to go, if you want to stay right here and board, then that's what we'll do. All I want is to be with you."

"Really?" I said.

He clenched his teeth and raised his hands pretending he was going to wring my neck. We both laughed.

"Yes, really, you psycho," he said.

We kissed right there on the edge of the big ramp, boarders flying back and forth behind us. Corey held me tightly, wrapping my grimy, sweaty self into his perfectly pristine suit. I had never felt so safe. He had picked me. It was really and truly over.

"Well, I *guess* we could go to the dance," I said, resting my forehead against his. "I mean, I did buy a dress and everything."

Corey pulled back, his beautiful green eyes wide. "Really? A dress? Now *this* I gotta see."

I flushed and whacked his arm, but before I could turn

away, he pulled me toward him for another kiss. My breath caught in my throat, and I smiled. "The dance can wait," he whispered.

As our lips touched, I couldn't have agreed more.

The End

(or not . . . turn the page!)

# The Choice Redux

*This* ending not happy enough for you? Well, if it's not, then your expectations are far too high, and I pity you for all the major disappointments you're going to endure in life. But, whatever, it is your decision, so if you think I can do better, go back to page 85 and choose a new man.

*Here's a sneak peek at*

# Hook Up *or* Break Up #2

# If You Can't Be Good, Be Good at It

"Cara, I need you to get over here. Like, now," I said into the phone.

It was Saturday. Valentine's Day. And it was already three o'clock. I had become the master procrastinator with a gold medal in avoiding phone calls. All it had taken was a couple of e-mails to Nate and Ian the night before, telling them I couldn't call back because I wasn't feeling well, and the phone had miraculously stopped ringing. I was a big, fat, liar. That was what a girl had to do when she was incapable of making decisions. And I was definitely incapable. Thus, the panicked phone call.

"What's wrong?" she asked.

"What's wrong? What's *wrong*?" I shouted, pacing my room in my bathrobe. Laid out on my bed were three outfits: Simple, sexy black dress for Nate, ripped jeans and tank for Ian, black slacks and sophisticated top for Drew. I had no idea which one I would be wearing. "What's wrong is I have three dates getting here in four hours."

"Three . . . three what?" Cara said weakly. "Wait a minute, I thought it was two."

"It *was* two," I said, throwing up my hand. "Until Drew asked me to his gallery opening yesterday and I said yes."

"Layla! Why? Why did you say yes?"

"Because! It was Drew Sullivan! And he kissed me! And I'd just . . . gotten a belly button piercing and I think all the adrenaline was messing with my brain," I said, putting my hand over my eyes and sitting down on my desk chair.

"You got a *what*? All right. That's it. I'll be right there."

The line went dead and I got up and flopped facedown on my bed on top of my jeans. Pain shot through my stomach and I flipped over, cursing my own stupidity.

How had I let it get this far? How, how, how?

"Okay, let's think about this logically," Cara said as I watched the minute hand on the kitchen clock move up a notch. Cara had shown up in her red V-Day dress, all coiffed and ready to go, her curly hair falling in sweet tendrils around her face. "You have to go with Nate. It's obvious."

"You only want me to go with Nate because then I'll be going to the dance with you," I said, leaning my elbows on the counter. "Besides, we don't know for sure that Nate even wants to go with me. He may have already heard all about me and Ian and me and Drew. I swear he was trying to break up with me yesterday."

"You don't know that for sure," Cara said.

"Call it women's intuition," I said grumpily.

"All right, so then it's Ian," Cara said with a shrug. "I mean, the guy is offering backstage passes to the Bloodworms and the potential to party with Necro. Hello? You've been fantasizing about that since fifth grade."

"I know. But is it fair to pick him because of what he can give me?" I said. "Isn't that kind of like using him?"

"Well . . . how do you feel about him?" Cara asked.

"I'm definitely attracted to him, but I'm not sure," I said, feeling desperate. "It might just be the mystique."

Cara groaned. "Okay, fine. Go with Drew then. God, you've wanted Drew since you were a zygote. It's totally obvious. Why are we even discussing this?"

"Because Nate is ridiculously sweet and Ian is ridiculously hot and exotic and I am just going to kill myself," I said, standing up. "So, what do you suggest I do, then?" I said.

"I suggest you be a woman," Cara said firmly, standing up straight and crossing her arms over her chest. "It's tough love time, my friend. I'm sorry, but you got yourself into this mess, Layla. Now you have to get yourself out of it. So decide. Who's it gonna be? The jock, the Brit, or the lifelong crush?"

"I don't know!" I wailed.

"Well you'd better decide and you'd better do it now," Cara said, glancing grimly at the clock. "Cuz you officially have less than an hour before your driveway is overflowing with guys. And that just ain't gonna be pretty."